A BLACK LEATHER CASE

A BLACK LEATHER CASE

by

Michael Cronin

Dales Large Print Books
Long Preston, North Yorkshire,
BD23 4ND, England.

British Library Cataloguing in Publication Data.

Cronin, Michael
    A black leather case.

    A catalogue record of this book is
    available from the British Library

    ISBN   978-1-84262-576-7 pbk

First published in Great Britain in 1971
by Robert Hale & Company

Copyright © Michael Cronin 1971

Cover illustration © Dax by arrangement with
P.W.A. International Ltd.

The moral right of the author has been asserted

Published in Large Print 2008 by arrangement with
Michael Cronin, care of Watson, Little Ltd.

Dales Large Print is an imprint of Library Magna Books Ltd.

Printed and bound in Great Britain by
T.J. (International) Ltd., Cornwall, PL28 8RW

ONE

Sam Harris was in bed with a bird, which was no new experience for him, except that this one was somewhat older than he normally chose. Myra was fifty, but in the right gear she could pass for forty in a dim light. In bed it was different, where the ravages of time couldn't be disguised, and it was Sam's conviction that he was doing her a favour, which is not a gentlemanly attitude.

She had picked him up three weeks earlier in a small drinking club near Baker Street, and she had made the running. She was a widow and she had money. And she needed a man.

Sam had never met a woman quite like her. She had style, and without saying anything she could somehow make Sam feel inferior, even in bed. She talked about stuff that was right over his head. Her legs were all right still, and she was more than okay for sex, but when it was over it was over, and he was to consider himself dismissed until she needed him again.

7

As now. She was asleep even before he got out of her bed. It wasn't what he was used to in his women. Sam liked to set the tone, and Myra acted like a bloody duchess with the second footman.

He smoked a cigarette, one of hers from the silver casket, and listened again to her slurry snoring into her pillow. She had this plush pad and more clothes than she could ever hope to drape around herself in a year crammed with social occasions. And the stuff there on her dressing-table would keep Sam in some degree of comfort for many a long month.

He was wondering, and not for the first time, just how he could put the bite on her. She had been costing him a bit here and there, because her notion of a merry evening wasn't a pie and a couple of gins in a pub. She had slipped him the odd fiver on occasion, but he was still out of pocket, and it was only right that a woman of her advanced years should expect to pay for her fun.

She grunted when he got out of bed. A contented cow. He began to dress, watching himself three-fold in the mirrors. Not a bad figure of a man, once he got his shirt and trousers on. Sharp. Neat. No belly. He brushed his crinkly hair with one of her silver-backed brushes, which she didn't like him doing. To hell with the old bag, she was asleep.

The emerald ear-rings she had been wearing winked at him from the glass top of the dressing-table. He shifted them around with the tip of one finger. Lovely stuff.

Myra papped her lips, grunted some more, and dug her face away into the pillow, her blue-rinsed hair covering her face. She knew she always looked like hell in bed afterwards.

Sam went over to the door of the bedroom and let himself out into the hall. One night he wasn't going to sneak off, he was going to stay put and see how she liked waking up with him beside her. Little old Sam, the widow's dream come true.

He was patting his tie in the hall mirror when he heard a noise from the floor above, a sharp crack like wood snapping, and a muffled shout. Somebody busting up the furniture.

There was a lot more noisy slamming around up there, and the thudding of feet. Sam opened the door, just a little. Myra always told him to make sure nobody saw him leaving, as if it mattered.

There was a fat little feller coming down the stairs, in a hurry, and he wasn't built for speed. He was carrying a black case and it didn't help because he had it in front of him, clasped to his chest. He missed the last few stairs, and flopped on his knees on the landing just in front of the lift.

The lift gates were closed and the lift was down on the ground floor. The man got to his feet and hobbled a few steps, painfully. He darted a quick worried look up the stairs. Then he hopped over to the landing window and put the case behind the curtains.

Sam watched him hobble to the next flight of stairs and start down, holding to the banister. His head was lowered, but Sam had seen his face, sweaty and worried; he was pretty nearly bald, but with thick dark eyebrows; he must have twisted an ankle, and he wasn't making much of a job on those stairs.

Sam listened, interested, but cautious. And a moment later he was glad he hadn't stuck his nose in because a door banged upstairs and a young man came bounding down, a very active young man who took those stairs four at a time and didn't make any fuss about it. He wore a roll-neck jersey, and there was a highly unfriendly look on his face.

From what Sam could see of it, the fat little feller was going to get himself clobbered before he got to the ground floor two flights below. The young man went past Sam's opening at speed, swung himself round the first bend and quickly out of sight, and very soon Sam was hearing the expected sounds of bodies in conflict below, the old grunts and stifled gasps.

He was about to come out and allow himself a closer view when he was aware of another man coming down those stairs at a sedate pace, a middle-aged man in a dark suit, walking with a stick; one stiff leg, carrying a black hat, his mouth thoughtfully set; frowning slightly. He stumped on down, in no hurry, and before he went out of Sam's view he put on the black hat.

Sam waited. The sounds of battle below had stopped. It couldn't have been much of a scrap. He tiptoed across to the landing window and lifted up the case. It was of black leather, a good one, with two locks. He shook it and knew it wasn't empty.

The little feller had a good reason for hiding it on his way down, and Sam didn't think he could have got very far, not with that young one after him. So the case was important. To all of them, and it would be plain daft to try to take it out of the building until he was sure they had all gone.

Sam did the obvious thing, he took the case back into Myra's hall. There was a cupboard where she kept odds and ends, in a corner by the phone; there was a bag of golf clubs that she didn't use any more, some rubber boots, old telephone books, junk like that. He tucked the case out of sight. He could pick it up whenever he liked. It just might show a profit.

If you kept on your toes plenty of unlikely things could show you a profit. That was Sam's experience. He shut the cupboard door. This was Wednesday, and he wasn't due to see Myra again until the Saturday night; she said she was going to be out stopping with some friends of hers in the country, Sussex or some place like that. It couldn't be better. Some time tomorrow, when it was all nice and quiet, he could get the case.

He lit a cigarette and let himself out of the flat. He stood and listened for a moment. It might be interesting to see what had happened below. He had descended three steps when he saw the legs on the flight above, moving down.

Then the hem of a skirt halfway up to

12

where it might be highly interesting. Sam was arrested. Nice legs always got him, and these were really good. The rest of the girl came into view. A dolly, in one of those shifts that look as though they have just been thrown on, or about to be taken off, casual, inviting speculation.

She was dark, with a small face and hair that brushed her shoulders. She inspected Sam, and smiled.

'Good evening,' she said.

'Evening,' said Sam. After the recent session with Myra his mind should have been on a higher plane.

The girl advanced towards him, and he retreated two stairs lower. He wasn't ready for this – attractive girls of her age didn't normally make this open approach to Sam, not when they were sober and in their right little minds. This one was sober all right.

'Are you going somewhere?' she asked softly.

'That's right,' said Sam.

'Don't go,' she said in a sharp little voice. 'I want to talk to you.'

'Sorry, I haven't got the time just now,' said Sam, preparing to move off.

'I found him up here,' said the girl, 'trying to sneak out.'

Sam looked down the stairs, and saw the middle-aged man with the limp coming up from the next landing. He was giving Sam the kind of rapid unpitying glance that Sam had seen so often from the bench when he was about to lose his liberty for a spell. Not encouraging.

'And what are you doing here?' the man demanded, swinging his stick.

'I'm going out, if it's any business of yours,' said Sam.

'Where have you come from? Quickly–'

'Just who the hell are you?' said Sam smartly. 'If you want to know, I've just come out of that flat back up there ... and now I'm leaving, see?' He could manage this cocky feller with the game leg and the dolly bird. The blasted nerve of some people.

The man stopped swinging his stick, he thrust it into Sam's middle. 'Up with you,' he said. 'Move.'

Sam shifted up one stair. The girl laughed softly. She had a small gun in one hand. 'I am a very good shot,' she said, and she was still giving him that come-on smile. 'Let's have you up here under the light.'

Sam was the filling in the sandwich. With that stick rammed into his side he retreated up to the landing.

'What the hell do you think you're up to?' he said.

The man stared at him and said nothing. He stumped past Sam and went over to the lift, peered down the lift shaft and fingered the metal grille.

'Too small,' said the girl quietly. She stood behind Sam, he could smell her perfume, and he didn't want any part of her just then.

The man crossed to examine the landing window, twitching the curtain to one side. The window was shut and the fastening was high up in the frame.

'He didn't have time to get at that,' said the girl. 'He must have done it between here and the ground floor.'

'Perhaps.' The man came over and stood thoughtfully in front of Sam.

'What's the trouble, squire?' said Sam. 'Lost something?'

'How long have you been out here? On this landing?'

'Who wants to know?' said Sam.

The stick rapped him sharply across the shins, so that he hopped around and swore.

'Silly little man,' said the girl. 'You must answer up nicely.'

'I've just come out,' said Sam sulkily, 'And you can keep that bleeding stick to yourself.'

'Search him, Sophie, he may be new,' said the man.

'Like hell she will,' said Sam indignantly. 'I don't have to stand for any more of this–'

'Quiet, not so much heat.' Sophie had rammed her gun into his back. 'Stand still.' She patted him expertly, in no ladylike manner, took out his wallet and handed it to the man. 'Stand over by the wall,' she said.

Sam obeyed and the meagre contents of his wallet were checked. 'I'm going to make a stink about this,' he said, 'you see if I don't.'

'I don't think you will,' said Sophie, smiling.

The man recited from Sam's driving licence: 'Mr Samuel Harris, 14 Passamore Place...'

'Correct,' said Sam. He had moved on since Passamore Place, because landladies like their rent regularly, and it was cheaper to move. He held out his hand and the wallet was returned. 'I'm pushing off now,' he said. 'I know you're not the police and I know you got no right to be doing this... I'm a respectable citizen, I am–'

'I wonder,' said the man. 'You might very well be a burglar, sneaking around here at this time of the night... I think we should make sure, don't you? Where did you say you'd come from?'

'In there,' said Sam shortly. 'Mrs Myra Foster's flat, she's a friend of mine.'

The girl gave a nasty little laugh. 'All right then,' said Sam. 'Ask her.'

The man nodded at Sophie and rang the bell. Nothing happened for a while, Sophie linked her arm under Sam's, making them all one cosy little party. 'So he's a lying bastard,' Sophie murmured, 'the place is empty.'

Sam reached forward and gave the bell three quick jabs followed by a long one, Sam's signal. 'She's in,' he said.

The door opened and Myra looked out. She wore a shimmering blue wrap, her eyes were still pouched with sleep, and her make-up was smeared. She was not a welcoming sight. She glared at Sam with much hostility.

'What the hell do you want?' she said. With even more open hostility she looked at Sophie clinging so snugly to Sam's arm.

'Do excuse the intrusion,' said the man, holding his black hat across his chest, 'but we found this man behaving rather suspiciously on the stairs, he says he's been visiting you.'

'You tell them, Myra,' said Sam, 'they won't believe me … they're trying to pretend they think I'm a burglar. You tell them

17

– I reckon they're a pair of nuts.'

'We do apologise for disturbing you at this late hour,' said the man, very politely.

Myra tightened her hold on her wrap, as though expecting an improper assault, and her gaze swept over Sam without the slightest sign of recognition.

'Myra, for Gawd's sake,' said Sam.

'Who is he?' she said frigidly.

Sam made strangled noises. Sophie was leaning against him more affectionately than ever. 'He says he knows you,' she remarked. 'His name is Samuel Harris.'

'How quaint,' said Myra, and her eyes began to glitter, so that Sam knew she was about to act the well-bred lady, the way she did with waiters and taxi drivers.

'Come on, Myra,' he said coaxingly, 'a joke's a joke, tell them who I am, I'm fed up with this.'

'What a very odd man,' said Myra. 'I can't think why he should say he knows me.'

'Marvellous,' said Sam bitterly. 'All right, you've had your fun, now put this pair of mugs right before I start shouting the place down–'

Myra shrugged and gave a thin smile. 'Quite ridiculous,' she said. As she was closing her door Sam said, with some venom,

'And you can get knotted.'

'What a nasty little fellow you are,' said Sophie. 'She disowned you.'

The lame man had been looking at Sam. 'I think we may have been making a small mistake. She knew him.'

'Damn right she did,' said Sam. 'She's just a bit coy about people knowing I spent the evening in her place, wait until I see her tomorrow, I'll tell her what I think of her–'

'–You already did,' said Sophie.

'Well if you've finished your mucking about,' said Sam, 'I'll be shifting along.'

'Essard,' said Sophie, 'we'd better let Ric Bonnard see him before we let him go.'

Sam glared impotently, first at Sophie, then at the man, Essard. 'Don't mind me,' he said, 'I reckon you must be crazy, both of you … what makes you think I'm going to let you push me around?'

Sophie reached forward, smiling. 'Good night,' she said.

Sam took her hand. She swung on her heel, and Sam was face-down on the carpet and the strain on his shoulder made him yelp. She held him there stiff-armed and rigid. Then effortlessly she yanked him to his feet.

'Are you coming, Mr Harris?' she said.

Without any further coaxing they took him down the rest of the stairs. They met nobody, after eleven at night the building was normally quiet. There were some shops on the ground floor, including an expensive florist's which was always tastefully lit; a glass-fronted arcade ran the width of the building, making a second entrance, but after business hours it was locked, as now.

They went out through the main swing doors. On the short drive-in at the front there was a black Mercedes.

Sam had been nursing his shoulder. 'Listen,' he said, 'I don't know what this is all about–'

'–We must hope you don't,' said Essard pleasantly.

A man emerged from the back seat of the car. He was the active young man Sam had seen in pursuit down the stairs.

'What have we here?' he said.

On the back seat Sam could see the head and shoulders of the fugitive – he was lolling back in a corner with his eyes shut and the street light gleamed on his pate. Sam began to feel distinctly uneasy.

'We found him on the stairs,' said Essard, 'and we thought he looked suspicious.'

'Bloody sauce,' said Sam, more defiantly

than he felt.

Bonner grinned. 'I've seen him around here before,' he said. 'He sleeps with the old chicken on the floor below us – am I right, old son?'

'I wouldn't put it like that,' said Sam stiffly. 'The lady happens to be a friend of mine.'

Sophie sniggered. 'He doesn't look much like a Casanova to me.'

Bonner drew Essard to one side, there was a whispered consultation, and they both looked at the front of the tall building.

'Seems we made a little boob,' said Sophie to Sam. 'No hard feelings?'

'You got some nasty habits,' Sam told her. 'They'll get you into bad trouble one day.'

Smiling, Sophie showed him the tip of her tongue. 'I don't need any gun to manage stuff like you.'

'Sophie, you wait in the car,' said Bonner, then he and Essard went back into the building.

Sam felt a little bolder. He lit a cigarette. 'What's the matter with that bloke in the car?' he said.

'A little under the weather,' said Sophie. 'You can go home now.'

'I reckon I ought to report this to the

police,' said Sam. 'I got quite a score against your lot – interfering with the liberty of a law-abiding citizen, offering threats, assault with intent to do grievous bodily harm... I don't reckon you got a permit for that gun. Come to think of it, I could make one hell of a stink.'

'You have your patter off right,' said Sophie. 'Very impressive. But if you are a law-abiding citizen I am the queen of Sheba. Nothing happened. Nothing you can now prove. Right? But if you're still hanging around when they come back, some of that grievous bodily harm stuff might just come true, Ric Bonner is rather impetuous.'

'You don't scare me,' said Sam. He backed off a few yards, to give himself room to manoeuvre if necessary. A little late traffic rolled past on the street.

'On your way, Samuel.' Sophie got into the back of the car and put her arm round the shoulders of the man inside, so that they looked like an oddly-assorted loving couple. With her free hand she waved Sam away. She was, he reflected, no ordinary bird.

There was no percentage in running up against those two again. That young Bonner was a right bastard, Sam was sure of that – and he had what they wanted, or he would have by tomorrow.

So that made them not so smart after all, Sam liked that. Maybe he didn't amount to much, maybe he scratched about for his bread and had to let tricky birds like that Sophie toss him around ... but if they only knew what he knew. He removed to a discreet distance, lit another cigarette and continued to savour the situation.

He had to leave his car in the nearby square, because Myra made a fuss if he parked outside the flat, as if it made any damn difference, probably everyone in the place knew he was bedding down with Myra, that Bonner, he knew right away. Sam grinned, Myra would bust her girdle if she knew people called her an old chicken. What a lousy trick, pretending she didn't know him.

'We'll check from our door to where I got him on the stairs,' said Bonner, leading the way in, much too fast for the limping Essard. 'There'll be a cupboard somewhere, some door we've been missing, a ledge or shelf, he only had a few seconds, and I could see him on the last landing – he had got rid of it by then, it's somewhere up there, it has to be.'

Essard clumped up the stairs, frowning. It

had been a disastrous evening, unexpectedly so. He was still seeing Voyses back to the door of the flat with the case under his arm, while the three of them had stood, motionless with Voyses swinging his gun to cover them – Voyses who had never been known to carry a gun before.

Sophie had been the one to make the first move, and Voyses had put a bullet into the wall beside her head, very deliberately, and some of the plaster Essard had felt stinging his face, so that he had only a confused picture of the end of it – Voyses tossing his gun into Bonner's face and then slipping out of the door. With the case.

Essard thought he knew why Voyses had abandoned his gun – he had been sure of his escape and he wouldn't want to run the risk of being with a gun on the street, not here in London. That was the way Voyses would think. But he had hurt himself on the stairs on the way down, he had been limping when Bonner jumped on him. Without the case.

All the carpeting was fitted, wall to wall, so he hadn't slipped the case under anywhere. Bonner had found just the one door unlocked, a cupboard, with brooms and cleaning stuff. All the other doors led to the

24

residents' flats. There were no convenient ledges where the case could have been propped out of sight. There were two tall curtained windows, one on each landing, both of them fastened, and if Voyses had been able to throw the case out of one of them they would have seen it outside by the drive-in, and Bonner was sure there hadn't been time for that.

'He didn't have it when I saw him,' he said. 'He was floundering about on the stairs...'

'Pity we let him jump us like that,' said Essard.

'You were there,' said Bonner shortly. 'I didn't notice you doing anything heroic.'

'It will make us look a little silly.' Essard's voice was mild.

'It'll do more than that,' said Bonner.

'Voyses is no gunman,' said Essard.

'Any man with a gun in his hand is a gunman,' said Bonner savagely. 'Ask Sophie. We're wasting time here. Voyses didn't perform any miracle, the case is here, he'll have to tell us where. Come on.'

Essard followed Bonner down the stairs. There would be a simple explanation, and Bonner would get it – and enjoy getting it. Essard could almost feel sorry for Voyses. Almost.

TWO

Sophie drove the Mercedes, with Essard sitting beside her. Bonner had Voyses on the rear seat. Voyses had now come round, but he was saying nothing and showing no interest in his surroundings, he was too much of a professional to hope for anything. He had tried something, on his own, he had nearly brought it off, and he knew if he made one unwise move Bonner would silence him for a long time. He had to keep his faculties about him.

The throbbing pain in the side of his neck where Bonner had chopped him down on the stairs was lessening; his wrenched ankle was far more painful – if that hadn't happened he thought he would have got clean away.

'Nearly did it, old son,' said Bonner. 'Nice try.'

'You came back too early,' said Voyses in a flat uninterested tone. They might have been discussing a minor social misdemeanour.

'This is one you're going to lose,' said

Bonner. Voyses closed his eyes and made no reply. He was having a small private thought – how pleasant it would have been if he had put a bullet into Bonner's belly, and what a difference it would have made. He wouldn't be riding with them now. He composed himself. He had made no plans for failure, and already his mind was beginning to speculate about the limits of bodily pain that a man might endure without breaking.

Bonner would be in a hurry to get what he wanted to know, so he would be crude, and Essard, the gentlemanly Hugo Essard, he would prefer to have nothing to do with Bonner's methods – he was much too civilised to enjoy breaking a man's body and then his spirit, but he would do nothing to stop it.

Sophie drove the car through the park and out into Knightsbridge. When a police car overtook them near Harrods Bonner gripped Voyses on the soft part of his thigh, stiffening his leg with the pain of it, and nobody had to say anything. They were three lucky men, as any impartial observer would have agreed. They were being driven home in an excellent car, and their driver was a highly attractive girl; perhaps one of them would be going to sleep with her, some men had that kind of luck. There was no justice.

Coming into Chiswick, the Mercedes turned down a quiet road near the river, and along a cobbled alley behind some large detached houses, Victorian and eminently respectable, family residences from the good old days when the golden sovereign chinked imperially and domestic help was dirt cheap.

Bonner got out and opened a pair of tall doors set in a high wall, and Sophie drove into a spacious garage with a clean concrete floor and the smell of new paint. And Voyses, who thought he knew all the addresses they were using, wondered how long they had had this one.

There would be plenty of room, it was quiet, handy both for London and the airport – obvious advantages. And the neighbours wouldn't bother them. It might well be their new operational headquarters, and he should have known about it ... so now he was going to find out about it the hard way, a sobering thought.

Bonner took him along a garden path, down a short flight of stone steps with iron railings, into a semi-basement which had once been the domestic area. There was a large room with two barred windows, a bright red bitumastic floor that didn't seem to have been walked on much, a large old-fashioned table with a scrubbed wooden top where meals for a score of hearty eaters could have been prepared. Where the old kitchen range used to be there was a gleaming electric stove, with an over-size refrigerator beside it. Between the two windows there was a new sink unit.

The lighting was harsh, and there was a chilly feeling in the air that suggested the room hadn't been recently in use; no lingering food smells.

Bonner shoved Voyses into a high-backed kitchen chair and grinned amiably at him. 'It's not much of a place but it's the best we can do at such short notice.'

Voyses glanced impassively around the room, while Bonner went over and closed the wooden shutters inside the two windows; his movements were brisk – he was going to enjoy what lay ahead.

Thoughtfully, Sophie stood and watched Voyses; she had her small automatic out but she knew she wasn't going to need it, not with Ric Bonner about.

'You will not be needing me,' said Essard, idly swinging his cane.

'I can think of nothing that you might do,'

said Bonner with undisguised contempt, 'except spew on the nice clean floor.'

'You are offensive,' said Essard, but conversationally still.

'I'm not a gentleman, I just earn my pay – tell Rass I want him, with some rope,' said Bonner, now very clearly the man in charge.

Essard went out and closed the door behind him. Sophie hoisted herself up on to the edge of the table and sat swinging her legs. She wasn't altogether sure how much of this she could take – she had never seen Bonner do anything, anything like this, but she had heard the talk about him, and it aroused a strange feeling inside her, sort of sexual mixed up with wanting to run away and hide.

'Now Voyses, old son,' said Bonner, pulling up a chair so that he sat knee-to-knee with Voyses, 'what is it going to be? It's your party exclusively this time. Do I bang it out of you or do I coax it out of you?'

Voyses had pale grey eyes. Sophie thought he looked harmless and very frightened; she knew he wasn't harmless. He had a little paunch that bulged defencelessly over the top of his trousers, and he was sweating heavily … over forty and not in good condition. Of course he was frightened.

She was willing him to speak, he hadn't a prayer now.

'Tell him,' she said softly. 'Tell him what you did with it, that's all he wants to know, isn't it, Ric? Then he can go back and tell them he couldn't get it, tell them it wasn't there, they won't know... Voyses, are you listening to me?'

'He's listening,' said Bonner.

'You should not use your women on this,' said Voyses. 'It is not fitting, and it is not civilised, if you know what I mean by that. Send her away.'

Bonner bent suddenly forward and caught Voyses by the fleshy part of each thigh, digging in with finger and thumb, pinning him to the chair, their faces a few inches apart.

'You don't make the rules here, my fat friend,' said Bonner. 'She stays if she wants to.'

Sophie had stopped swinging her legs, suddenly uneasy about the display she was putting on when she found that Voyses had shifted his untroubled gaze to her.

'Go,' he said quietly. 'It should not interest you.'

She slid off the table, Bonner laughed and poked Voyses hard and viciously in the stomach.

31

'Time is passing,' said Bonner. 'What did you do with the case? Where did you put it?'

Voyses stared over Bonner's shoulder. Now his world was bounded by the limits of this room. This was far from being his first 'interrogation' – the bent fingers of his left hand were reminders of a previous experience, but he had been younger then, more resilient. He wondered how long he could endure now, how soon his body might betray him.

'You know I will tell you nothing,' he said, his lips barely moving.

'Ric,' said Sophie, 'there must be another way … he's a sensible man, he must know when he's beaten…'

'His kind never knows,' said Bonner. 'Look at him sweating…'

'It just seems a pity,' she said slowly.

'Take your pity upstairs, it won't do him any good here,' said Bonner.

At the door she met Rass coming in, and as usual he looked right through her, without making room for her to pass, so that she had to sidle out into the corridor. She went upstairs to wait with Hugo Essard, and now that Rass was there it wouldn't be a long wait.

Rass wore black tights and a loose white blouse with no sleeves, he had the lithe figure of a ballet dancer, except for the muscularity of his long arms and heavy development of his chest. From the waist down he was compact and supple, and his movement was an effortless glide. Quite hairless, he was an even light brown from the gleaming top of his narrow skull down to his tiny feet of which he was inordinately proud.

He claimed to be a native of Famaka on the Blue Nile, but the likelihood was that he had more of Ethiopia in him than the Sudan, with his narrow nose and thin mouth. He was practically tireless, and very inventive about methods of treating the human frame, male and female, and very few women, even seasoned professionals, were anxious to spend more than one night in his company.

In one hand he held a coil of nylon rope. His voice had a eunuch's treble, which added piquancy to some of his more eso-teric bedroom exploits.

'This one not talking?' he said. 'How quick you want him talking?'

'Pretty quick,' said Bonner. 'But not too messy. Let's get him on the table first–'

33

Rass wound one arm around Voyses and lifted him out of his chair, and slammed him down on the table on his back, like a butcher handling a side of beef. He held him down, with one hand on his windpipe. Bonner took the rope and fastened it round the legs of the table, and wound it tight around Voyses, so that Voyses could move nothing but his eyelids. When he tried to move his head Rass tightened his fingers and cut off his breathing.

'We warm him a little,' said Rass. 'Then he talk good.'

Bonner bent over Voyses. 'You heard that ... do you want your feet fried?'

Voyses closed his eyes. Rass pulled off his shoes and socks, went over to the stove and plugged in the electric iron. On the shelf over the sink there was a transistor radio, he fiddled about until he got a music pro-ramme ... he could remember getting some excellent results with electrodes on the priv-ate parts of an obstinate subject to the haunting swing of 'The Blue Danube', not many weeks ago.

He turned the volume up, tested the iron, and unplugged it. Holding Voyses' feet, each in turn, he applied the iron, lightly at first. Voyses arched his back, quivering, wagging his head from side to side, while Bonner bent and listened for what he wanted to hear.

It took Rass thirty-five seconds and two full applications of the iron to have Voyses screaming high above the music, and Rass nodded his approval. It was going well. Then he held the iron over Voyses' eyes, ramming his head hard down on the table.

Bonner turned the music down. 'Talk,' he said. 'Talk, you fool.'

'Very soon,' said Rass. He went over and plugged the iron in again. There was a silence in the room, except for the quick noisy breathing of the man on the table. The smell was sickening. Rass didn't notice it, but Bonner had to light a cigarette.

Bending over Voyses, he said impatiently: 'You might as well talk now ... you're just being stupid–'

Voyses' mouth twisted, and he spat into Bonner's face. But he said nothing. The scorched soles of his feet had spread his toes and the sweat ran down his grey face. He was no longer straining at the rope that bound him. He couldn't see Rass, but he knew what he was about to do. He could feel his heart hammering, and the sharpness that stabbed through his head ... it would not be long.

Rass brought the iron over, held Voyses' head down and singed his forehead, the merest touch, and again, lower down and nearer the eyes. Bonner turned away.

'Landing ... window...' said Voyses in a small high voice, and Bonner came back to bend over him. 'Say that again – which landing? Tell me ... Voyses, which landing?'

There was no answer, he shook Voyses stupidly, unable to move more than his head. 'I think the bastard's passed out on us.'

With his thumb Rass rolled an eyelid back. 'Feeling nothing,' he said, disappointed. 'I burn him some more later, okay?'

'He wouldn't be trying to fool us, not at this stage,' said Bonner, 'there wouldn't be any point in it.'

'Talking the truth,' said Rass professionally. 'Everybody the same when they get scared about their eyes.'

'I'll go back and make another search,' said Bonner. 'I must have missed something ... if you can get him talking some more, Rass ... we're looking for a black leather case that he hid somewhere on a staircase ... if I come back here without it we'll burn him into little pieces...'

'Can do,' said Rass, and Bonner hurried out of the room to report upstairs. Rass waited for some minutes, he heard the car back out of the garage, but nobody came down to join him, they seldom did on these occasions.

Later he undid the waistband of Voyses trousers and pulled them down with the top of his pants to expose his belly. He regretted that it was not a beautiful woman he was attending to, a young white woman with blonde hair for preference. There was no respiratory movement that he could detect; he felt for a heartbeat, and could feel none. Very disappointing, they had assured him this would be a tough one, worthy of his skill.

He heated the iron again, really heated it, and applied it to the middle of the belly. Nothing. Not a quiver. Exit Voyses. There would be some shouting upstairs over this. Rass put the iron away and gave himself a long cool drink of water. They should bring him better quality stuff to work on if they wanted results. It was a waste otherwise. A black leather case, that had been lost tonight – Rass was hoping they would find it.

Some two hours later Bonner burst into the room. 'The lying little bastard,' he said.

'Wake him up, Rass, and let's get to work properly!'

'Dead,' said Rass. 'No talk any more, that one.'

'You mean you didn't get any more out of him?'

'You ever hear of a dead man talking?' said Rass. 'Not a word out of him after you leave … this one not so tough.'

'Hell,' said Bonner thoughtfully, 'I didn't think he had the nerve to go on fooling us right to the end … he was tough enough, damn him.' He stared malevolently down at the lifeless figure on the table. Rass had removed the rope, only the shoes and socks were still missing. Voyses looked peaceful and small, shrunken almost.

'Have you told the Doctor?' said Bonner.

'I stay here,' said Rass. 'I don't mess with the Doctor. What we do with this one?'

'Dump it somewhere while it's still dark, you'll have to get into some clothes, Rass. Check his pockets, don't leave anything on him, okay? And cover up those goddam feet…' Bonner went out without looking again at the table. It would have suited him to tell Rass to handle the body on his own, but he knew Rass wouldn't wear that. Nor would Doctor Apian. Upstairs.

Doctor Aristide Apian was thirty-nine years old, handsome, alert, and full of confidence in his own ability. The son of a middle-class Syrian merchant and an ambitious French mother, Apian had taken his Doctorate with considerable distinction after post-graduate study at the Yale Law School. He had also won something of a reputation in collegiate circles as a sprinter ... and as a forceful and impassioned debater on social and political themes.

Now all that was well behind him, including the practice of Law. The people who counted in his world were beginning to take note of him as an organiser, and very soon, he confidently surmised, he would control the whole of the European operations of the underground United Arab movement.

The hi-jacking of a few airliners and the planting of ineffectual bombs on Israeli premises – Aristide Apian would make a more significant contribution when the time came, and very soon now.

In cream silk pyjamas that showed off his swarthy good looks, he sat up in bed, reading *The Death Of a President* – he was finding Manchester's exhaustive book absorbing, for a number of reasons, mostly because it demonstrated how ridiculously easy it was to remove a popular leader by violence when the conditions were right. All those battalions of allegedly expert agents and trained bodyguards had been defeated by one man with a gun. It had been done in Dallas, and it could be done elsewhere. London, for instance.

Officially Apian was accredited as a Cultural Attaché, which he found quite laughable. It was the most obvious cover imaginable, but it had never been questioned, and it allowed him liberty of movement, and almost unlimited funds. He had never been photographed by the press, and he was sure that so far nobody in London on the other side had a file on him.

He had listened to Bonner's recital. 'He hoodwinked you,' he said. 'There will be a simple explanation, Bonner, and you must find what it was before it is too late. An accomplice–'

'Voyses always worked alone,' said Bonner. 'We know that.'

'He changed the pattern,' said Apian. 'There was somebody else – the man whom you met on the stairs.'

Bonner shook his head doubtfully. 'We

checked him thoroughly.'

'You think you did, and you let him go,' said Apian. 'You have his name and you know his address, so even you should be able to pick him up. Take Rass with you, if you feel it is beyond you.' Apian's smile underlined the insult.

'I can manage without that – that nigger.'

'Nigger?' said Apian softly, 'does that make you feel better? Any less of a white Caucasian renegade?'

'He's too conspicuous, that's all I meant,' said Bonner. 'People will remember him.'

'So all Londoners are a muddy pink, like you?' said Apian politely. 'An interesting obsession, but not very helpful in the circumstances … never let me hear you talk that way when Rass might hear you.'

'What about Voyses?' said Bonner sullenly.

'A pity he could not be kept alive long enough to say what you needed to hear,' said Apian. 'If a similar situation arises, my dear Richard Bonner, do let me know before it is too late. A corpse is embarrassing in this country.'

'I thought Rass and I ought to get rid of it first,' said Bonner, anxious to please.

'By all means,' said Apian. 'Then this Harris fellow, bring him here, with or without

41

the help of Rass.'

Bonner nodded. He couldn't help himself glancing at the door which led, he knew so well, to the room where Sophie was. And he was going to spend the rest of the night ditching a corpse, with Rass ... and then he had to find that little ginger headed fornicator, Mr Samuel Harris.

Apian took up his book. 'Good hunting,' he said, smiling. 'I believe that is the expression you English use?'

Bonner went out. Apian read for a few minutes, but for once the book failed to engage his attention. It was twelve minutes past three. He could sleep. Or go next door. He could do both.

He got out of bed and slipped off his pyjamas. He inspected himself in the long mirror. It was still the body of an athlete. Lean and hard. A man's body, and already interested ... why not? He went next door, and turned on the bedside light.

He stood for a moment by the bed, while Sophie slowly came awake and turned her face to him.

'Not again,' she said drowsily... 'don't you ever get tired?'

'Tiredness is for old men,' he said. 'And I am not yet an old man, remember?'

'So how could I ever forget?' she said sleepily.

He turned back the single sheet and slid in beside her. She remembered.

THREE

Voyses had been carrying nothing with him that might identify him, and they didn't even have to do anything to his clothing; Rass had put his shoes and socks on, and Rass himself wore a nondescript grey suit. They dumped the body in the back of the Mercedes, and Bonner drove, because Rass was not very good with a car – he was quite likely to drive through a red light, and the last thing they wanted was to attract the attention of any roving squad car.

Bonner drove south, with much circumspection, and out on to the Chertsey bypass; there was little about. Just beyond Chertsey, near Thorpe, Bonner turned into a lane that led to a hilly copse with plenty of undergrowth, and no houses nearby. He found a gate, with the warning: 'Private. Trespassers will be prosecuted.'

They carried the body in among the waist-high bracken in the greying light; they disturbed some sleeping birds in the branches overhead; Bonner found a good spot, and they rolled the body under and well out of sight, clear of any path.

'I fancy he won't be bothering anybody for a long time,' said Bonner. 'Much safer than the river.'

They went back down to the car. The lane was too narrow for the Mercedes to turn. Bonner remembered that there was a farm of sorts at the bottom of the lane, it led nowhere else. It was now close on five o'clock, and farmers were early risers, so it mightn't be wise to drive down that far and run the risk of the car being remembered about. So he did a long and tiresome reverse. Then back up to London, and Samuel Harris.

Passamore Place was a short street of terraced houses in Kennington, shabby three-storeyed houses with iron railings in front and semi-basements; a lodging-house district, run-down and due for clearance. Number 14 looked no better than the rest.

Bonner didn't think it looked very promising. He made Rass stay in the car, and went up the steps and rang the bell. He couldn't hear it ringing inside, and he felt pretty sure that there would be more than one occupant.

There could be a dozen of them, four or five families perhaps, it was that type of place. The Mercedes didn't look right, squatting down there on the road. It was twenty to six, and the early workers would soon be about, and that car would arouse comment. He rang again, waited, then hammered with the knocker and heard it booming inside.

Presently a light came on below, in the basement, and the area door opened. A woman looked up at him. She had a mess of grey hair, and she wore a man's overcoat over her nightdress.

'What's the idea?' she said. 'Don't you know what bleeding time it is? You wanta wake the whole bleeding street?'

'I'm sorry,' said Bonner–

'–And so you ought to be … whaddya want at this time of the night?'

'I'm looking for Mr Harris–'

'–Mister,' said the lady, 'if you find him you might let me know, the bastard skipped owing six weeks rent.'

'I'm sorry,' said Bonner. 'I suppose you don't know where he's gone?'

'If I did he wouldn't be owing me rent,' she said with some venom. 'You a friend of his, mister?'

'Not exactly,' said Bonner. In a minute

46

she'd be expecting him to pay the arrears. 'But I do want to contact him.'

'Me too … g'night.' The area door slammed.

Bonner got back into the car and lit a cigarette. He hadn't really expected any result and he wasn't unduly disappointed. This was just the beginning. The woman, Mrs Myra Foster, she would have her boy friend's current address, even though she had pretended she didn't know him.

Bonner lived on the floor above, and he had seen Harris often enough. At a more respectable hour he would have to think up a story for Mrs Myra Foster. It might be a good idea to leave it to Hugo Essard, chatting up the older birds was one of his things. He started the car. Rass had heard the dialogue. He grinned, showing sharp pointed teeth. 'Smart feller, that one,' he said.

'Not all that smart,' said Bonner.

'Man, I never heard of no Harris before … where they bring him in from?'

'I don't think they did bring him in,' said Bonner. 'I think Voyses was on his own.'

'But the Doctor don't think the same like you,' said Rass, 'and he the boss.'

'I'll find Harris,' said Bonner, 'just to

47

prove I'm right. We'll drive to my place, and you can take the car back.'

'So what I gonna tell the boss?'

'He'll be asleep, he won't be expecting a report.'

Rass gave one of his high-pitched yuk-yukking laughs, to indicate that he knew how Aristide Apian had been engaged while they got rid of a dead body and looked for a man who wasn't there.

As a small girl, too young even to understand what was happening around her because she had never known anything else, Ilse Spolnyki had lived through the destruction of Warsaw, which had engulfed her parents and her few relatives. Along with the thousands of others like herself, she had drifted from one camp for DPs to another, growing older and wiser to the degrading ways of the world she found herself in. It had been a pilgrimage of despair, during which she met little kindness and less Christian charity.

She had nobody to speak for her but herself, so it was not surprising that she grew up tough in spirit, suspicious and guarded in her dealings with those who came across her. Nobody was going to drag her down, make an animal of her, like those others, and she met no man to whom she would willingly surrender her maidenhood, or any part of herself.

She had evaded intended rape on more than one occasion, by the unexpected fierceness of her resistance ... there were always more amenable bodies to be found in the huts of the camps and the ruined cities, and Ilse had little to recommend her except that she was female. She had grown into a lean and sinewy woman, hardened by labour and the daily battle for existence.

She knew she would never be thought beautiful, and it bothered her not at all, as long as she could remain mistress of herself and her way of life. Beauty was a luxury outside her world, like having more money to spend than you needed for your food each day. She had no religious beliefs, and she should have been ready-made fodder for the Communist propagandists who infested the camps where she had to spend so many of her early years, but even the most persuasive of them got nowhere with her.

She was twenty-nine when she got to London, with the help of a Red Cross official who had taken an interest in her, and who knew this was a young woman with more than ordinary character, not just another piece of human flotsam.

Employment was found for her with a family in Finchley, nominally as a domestic help, and probably for the first time in her life Ilse knew a measure of real contentment. She discovered a talent for cooking and running a household, and being surrounded for once with genuine friendliness drew her out of her defensive shell – nobody here was trying to take anything away from her.

She began to take an interest in her appearance, she put on some weight, which she could well afford, and there were times when she could appear almost pretty. In her free time she picked up typing and shorthand, because now she didn't intend to spend the rest of her life in a kitchen.

Then she met Harry Voyses, a middle-aged widower with few resources and evidently not much of a future, self-employed as an agent or contact man in some vague capacity with some firms abroad, mostly in the Middle East; Harry never told her precisely what he did, but she understood that he had seen better days.

They went through a sedate courtship, and six months after their first meeting Ilse

Spolnyki became Mrs Harry Voyses. They had a small flat in Clapham, where Harry had been living in a bachelor's muddle. Within a few weeks Ilse had changed all that, and she had also contrived to get herself a part-time job in an estate agency – they needed the money, because Harry's earnings were often irregular.

Very soon she knew that his work had some kind of a political side, which involved some travelling and meeting people at odd hours – he was a collector of information on a free-lance basis, all manner of information, he told her, and even to herself she never thought of him as a spy. That it might conceivably be dangerous she hid from herself – he always insisted that nothing could happen to him.

Before leaving that night he had assured her that he was on to something big … she could think about that washing machine and new curtains, and a holiday for the two of them. He would be home before midnight.

She was not unduly worried when he didn't come back. He had been late before, but as the night hours passed she couldn't sleep, and the bed was so empty. They had a phone and he would have rung her if something had come up to delay him.

She was preparing a solitary breakfast after a sleepless night when the phone rang and her heart lightened.

'I would like to speak to Mr Voyses, please.' It was a man's voice, curt and businesslike.

'He's not here ... can I take a message?'

'Do you know where I can get in touch with him? You are Mrs Voyses?'

'I'm Mrs Voyses,' she said. 'I'm afraid I don't know where he is, not at the moment...'

There was a pause. 'But you expect him back soon, I take it?'

'Yes,' she said, 'any minute now.'

'Ask him to ring me as soon as he comes in, will you, please?'

The 'please' came very much as an afterthought and didn't mean a thing.

'Who shall I say called?'

'He'll know, Mrs Voyses.' The caller rang off.

She sat at the kitchen table, letting her coffee grow cold, and now she couldn't pretend that she wasn't more than just uneasy. She was due to go to work in half an hour, but she couldn't go out, she had to wait and be there when he returned. She rang the firm and told them she wasn't well and wouldn't be in until later. Then she sat and waited.

She couldn't just sit. She started on her housework, but that still left her with un-consumed time on her hands. The caller rang again, at half past ten, more abruptly than before. No, she said, her husband was still out ... and she hadn't heard from him.

'You stay in, Mrs Voyses, I'm coming to see you. Understand? Don't go out.'

It was an order. She would have told him to go to hell, but this concerned Harry. 'I'll be here,' she said.

Sam Harris had an unpleasant shock when he arrived to do his little breaking-and-entering on Myra's flat. He had waited until after ten to give her time to be on her way for her country visit, and he proposed to be in and out of the building in a couple of minutes. With that case.

He was coming happily through the main door when he saw a man emerging from the florist's with a sheath of yellow roses in his hand, looking very courtly and elegant, limping and carrying a stick, and heading for the stairs.

Sam reversed smartly out. Gawd, would you credit it ... he had almost walked right into it. Lucky it hadn't been that Ric Bonner bloke, he wouldn't have missed Sam, and then there might have been more of the awkward stuff like last night.

Sam slipped into a nearby coffee bar. He didn't like near-misses, they loused things up. He would have to make sure that he didn't bump into any more of that mob upstairs, and that went for the dolly Sophie as well, with her little heater. He had thought a lot about the feller he had seen on the back seat of that Mercedes ... and he doubted very much if he had passed a peaceful night, unlucky bastard. All of which made that case worth conniving for – it might even be loaded with hot gear, there had been some handy jewellery snatches recently that had put the fuzz in a right tizzy.

It would be a bit of all right if little Sam had tripped over some of that stuff. The big thing now was to be invisible while he got his hooks on it.

He waited half an hour, then rang Myra's flat from a call-box.

'What was the game last night?' he said. 'Pretending you didn't know me–'

'–Oh Sam,' she said gushingly, 'wasn't it awful of me? But really I didn't know what to think when I saw you standing there with those people... I mean, they might have been police or anybody – and I do hate gossip... I must have lost my head – are you terribly cross at me?'

'I'm not laughing much,' he said. 'You didn't have to drop me in the dirt like that ... anybody would think you were ashamed of me–'

'–You know me better than that, Sam,' she said reproachfully.

'Do I?'

Myra muffled the receiver against her breast and smiled across at the courtly gentleman – he had brought her roses and a charming apology for disturbing her last night.

'It's Sam,' she explained. 'I'm afraid he's rather angry about last night.'

'Ask him over,' said Hugo Essard. 'I really would like to make things right with him, Mrs Foster – it was unpardonable of me ... do ask him...'

Myra shrugged. 'If you like.' She could hear Sam's muffled squawks against her left breast. There had been no need for her to admit that she knew Sam, and Hugo Essard's manner suggested that she was so desirable that any little feminine foible could be forgiven her.

'Sam,' she said.

'You got somebody there with you?' he demanded.

'Well yes,' she said, 'somebody who's very anxious to meet you, actually – are you coming over to see me off, Sam?'

'Not bloody likely,' said Sam with no originality. 'Have a nice trip.' And he rang off.

'Oh dear,' said Myra, putting the phone down. 'He's quite upset.'

There was nothing on Hugo Essard's face to indicate what he was thinking. The stupid woman had bungled it.

'Never mind,' he said smoothly. 'Perhaps you could let me have his address, then I could call on him and put things right... We were frightfully clumsy last night.'

Myra thought this was carrying good manners too far.

'Do you think that's really necessary?' she said.

'Please,' said Essard with a charming smile. He was seething inwardly.

'Porchester Walk,' said Myra. 'He has a flat or rooms ... I've never been there, of course – number 14b, I think he said.'

'Very kind of you,' said Essard, getting to his feet. 'I gather you're going away, Mrs Foster?'

Myra smiled and nodded, walking him to the door. 'Until the end of the week.'

'I do hope we'll meet again,' he said politely. 'I often visit a neighbour of yours on the floor above.'

'Do look in when you're passing.' Myra had already begun to think that he might have possibilities. He was nearer her own age, evidently a gentleman – and he was interested, she was sure of that. It would make a pleasant change from Sam, who really couldn't be taken anywhere decent. Hugo Essard, company director – that limp gave him a distinguished air, she thought, and he was probably highly sexed, cripples were supposed to be...

Half-way through her packing she remembered the golf clubs she had promised to bring with her, as a present for the daughter of the house – a great lumpy girl who thought of nothing but ponies and whacking golf balls about. The clubs were as good as new.

What a damn nuisance, lumbering herself with them. But she had promised, and there'd be one of those frightful fusses if she arrived without them – teenage girls were hell.

She looked for the clubs, aimlessly. She

hadn't used them for years – hearty outdoor exercise wasn't Myra's thing. She remembered the hall closet. As she dragged the bag out the leather case fell into view. She picked it up. Odd, she couldn't remember putting it there, and she knew it wasn't hers – it wasn't the kind of thing she'd ever have any use for. It was a man's business case, and a good one. It might well have been in that closet for months.

It was a puzzle, and she tried to think whose it might be. There was Freddie Furnivall, he had been something of a visitor at one time, until his wife got suspicious. He had been something in the Civil Service. A hush-hush job, he always hinted. She could remember that he had once or twice arrived with a case, but not like this one, and he had always been fussy about having it with him – part of his alibi, or excuse for working late.

She tried to undo the locks with a nail file, but gave it up and pushed the case into the top of her wardrobe, behind her discarded hats. She'd get it open somehow, when she had more time.

Ilse looked at the young man standing at her door, and her first impression was that he couldn't have been the one who had phoned her so abruptly. He looked like the kind of polished young man who would have an executive position in a superior fashion house … something artistic, decorative. His clothes were good and expensive – the kind of clothes Harry could never hope to wear. A big young man. Swarthy, not quite hand-some, one day he might be fat, but not yet.

'Mrs Voyses? I rang you – may I come in? I am Leo Grussmann.'

'I'm afraid my husband isn't here,' she said, but she held the door open. Leo Grussman? Harry seldom mentioned names, and she was certain she had never heard of this one before.

In the little sitting-room he appeared bigger than ever, more glossy, more obvi-ously prosperous, a young man who had arrived somewhere important, she thought. So what possible connection could he have with Harry? It frightened her. And she couldn't explain why, yet.

'Mrs Voyses,' he said, 'I do regret having to bother you like this, but it is important.'

'Of course,' she said. 'Do sit down.' This was still her house. She would set the terms of their discussion. She sat opposite him with her hands primly folded in her lap. He was not from the police. She needn't be frightened.

He gave her a smile which she didn't return. 'Well?' she said. 'I don't know you, Mr Grussmann. What do you want?'

'I would like to talk to you about your husband,' he said. 'I had a business arrangement with him. He was to meet me last night, but he failed to arrive, so I am naturally concerned. What time did he go out last night, Mrs Voyses?'

'Have you any right to ask that?' she said. 'Does my husband have to account to you for his movements?'

Grussmann smiled again, this time a genuine smile. 'When I meet your husband I must remember to congratulate him on the loyalty of his wife. Mrs Voyses, last night your husband was employed by me, I paid him an advance on his commission ... he did not talk to you about it?'

'No.'

He knew she was telling the truth. She would lie when she had to, but not over this.

'Are you thinking my husband has cheated you? You cannot know him very well.'

'Where is he?' said Grussmann in a surprisingly gentle voice. 'You were expecting him back last night but he didn't come. And you haven't heard from him since, have you?'

'No.' The truth again. There was fear behind those eyes of hers, and he knew it wasn't fear of him.

'You are worried about him, Mrs Voyses, and so am I. We are both concerned.'

'He is my husband,' she said. 'What was this thing you had paid him to do?'

'I am not at liberty to give you the details,' he said. 'It was a delicate matter.'

'You mean dangerous,' she said.

'Perhaps.'

She looked at him with undisguised contempt. 'You are a young man, you appear healthy – why did you not do this delicate thing yourself? Why make use of my husband?'

'Mrs Voyses,' he said earnestly, 'it was not like that, believe me – how much do you know of your husband's business?'

'Enough,' she said stolidly. 'You say you employed him – to do what?'

'It was information,' he said. 'He knew where he could get it, and I needed it. It was his suggestion … and it required a skill that I do not have. It was a business arrangement.'

'Information about what?' she said. 'You are telling me nothing.'

He stood up. 'I'm sorry – perhaps I know your husband better than you think … he was an honest man.'

Her thin face tightened. 'Why do you say "was"? You know something has happened to him – you must tell me–'

'I don't know,' he said. 'He has worked for me before, Mrs Voyses, and nothing has gone wrong, until now.'

'Until now,' she repeated bitterly, 'and it is now that matters … so where is he? Where is my husband?'

'I wish I knew,' he said.

She followed him out to the door, like a woman walking in a dream, a nightmare. In a choked voice she said, 'my husband would never cheat you … you may think what you please.'

'If he doesn't ring me I'll see you again,' he said quietly, and it was no threat.

When he had gone she shut the door and wished she could sit and weep. But that wouldn't help Harry.

FOUR

Sam Harris had temporarily abandoned his observation on Myra's flat. Much later would have to do for that. Give her plenty of time to get out and on her way for that country visit. Silly bitch. Trying to play him for a sucker, him, Sam Harris – inviting him to call and get himself clobbered!

He was driving down the cobbled entrance under the archway to Porchester Walk, and as he was turning the last sharp corner on the slope by the railings he jammed his brakes on and there wasn't even time to swear.

Parked outside the faded door of number 14b, there was a car, which was nothing out of the ordinary – but lounging by this car, with a paper in his hand, there was the unwelcome figure of Ric Bonner.

Sam first thought of a rapid reverse back round the corner and up the slope, but he was in too much of a hurry and scraped his gears with some nasty noises, which drew Bonner's attention away from his newspaper, and he knew Sam right away even as Sam began to scramble out. He grinned.

'Hi, Samuel,' he called out.

Sam darted up the slope. The pub on the corner wasn't his local, he hadn't been there long enough yet, but he knew the layout. Controlling his mad dash, he pushed the saloon bar door open and walked across to the door opposite. There was only a small midday crew of boozers, and the barman was doing something out of sight under the bar, showing nothing but a slice of his vast rump. Nobody greeted Sam as he slid nonchalantly out into the corridor leading to the Gents, and the yard at the side.

A couple of bouncy strides took him into the yard. The crates were in the right place, stacked against the wall, so Sam was up and over that wall and in the messy garden next door.

There were tired old stunted trees, sooty grass, and a broken frame of a greenhouse. There was a back gate that would lead into the lane, and that was just where Bonner would be waiting for him, he thought. Perhaps Bonner hadn't seen him duck into the pub, but he would work that out once he didn't see Sam up the road beyond the arch.

Sam scuttled under a clothes line hung

with kid's stuff, by the window he could see a pram, and the house was probably bulging with tenants and kids. While he hesitated he saw a young woman come out and bend over the pram! She was too busy making goofy noises at her kid to notice Sam down at the end of the garden … but if she did see him she'd probably raise one hell of a fuss – never mess with a woman when she has a baby – they scream the place down.

He'd need to put a couple more gardens between him and the pub. There were a lot of windows watching him from the back of the houses. He got over the wall and found the next garden an improvement on the other – he could even hear radio music from one of the open windows. But nobody looked out yet and shouted at him.

More of the bloody Grand National lark. He was squatting on the next wall surveying the terrain, when he glanced back, and Ric Bonner, astride the first obstacle, waved at him in friendly fashion, and jumped agilely down, coming after him – and sure to catch him now.

Sam dropped into a garden where somebody had been doing some work – he had to pad through lines of pale green lettuce plants to get to the path, and some dead straight rows of early carrots. Down the path to the back door.

He tapped and found it unlocked and let himself into a corridor with broken linoleum. There was a smell of mince and onions. Through an open doorway he saw a little old lady sitting by a table, with her skirt hoisted and her feet in a basin. She hardly looked up as he passed. Having trouble with her bunions. All by herself.

Four steps up and there was the hall and the front door. There was a pram against the wall, and he could hear women talking on the floor above.

He could nip through the front door, which was what Bonner would expect him to do. Outside there was a long straight bit of road, and he'd have to run like hell if he hoped to outspeed Bonner ... with no cover. That would be asking for it, just what Bonner would be hoping for.

Sam knew his limitations. In front of him there was the cubby-hole under the main stairs. He checked it, plenty of room. He opened the front door and banged it shut – Bonner would have heard it. As he crept into the cubby-hole he heard the old lady's voice raised in querulous protest, and Bonner's cheerful: 'Okay ma ... just passing through.'

Sam blew a silent raspberry when Bonner's nimble footsteps sounded just a few inches away, and then there was again the boom of a slammed front door.

The array of gas meters ticked over his head. Sam made himself comfortable; there were heaps of old newspapers and some clothes that made a cushion of sorts; there was a smell of paraffin, which put him off trying a cigarette. After about ten minutes he heard the door bang but the steps were those of a woman, going up.

He thought about Myra who had given them his address, it must have been her ... you wouldn't believe that a woman who called herself a lady could be such a cow. He was adding up a solid score against Myra. Some footsteps shuffled past, accompanied by grumblings ... 'bleeding men think they own the place...' That would be the old lady with bad feet.

He allowed it another twenty long minutes. The hall was quiet when he emerged. He opened the front door. There were parked cars, but not Ric Bonner's. Sam catfooted it down the road, watching all ways at once. Porchester Walk was going to be out for an indefinite period; there was his car, not yet paid for by any means, with the keys ready for the first smart boy to lift it. And all because Myra couldn't keep her trap shut.

He caught a bus down to Marble Arch, in no pleasant or charitable frame of mind. In the pub off the corner of Edgware Road he had a light ale and a crab sandwich. And began to think of an alternative plan about that case, because he was now more convinced than ever that whatever that case held it was red hot to somebody ... they thought Sam knew something about it, so they were chasing after him. That made enough sense to Sam.

It was no new experience to him to be sought for, and by experts more than once, and he didn't think this new lot could be all that smart – keeping tabs on Myra's flat and Porchester Walk at the same time would take manpower. So he could wait and let them get tired.

Sam looked the bar over, there weren't any chicks worth his attention, but there was somebody he knew – Chopper Roberts watching him over the top edge of his midday paper, from a table by the door. Chopper lifted a finger, Sam nodded, and Chopper came over.

He was a slight insignificant man, just about as ordinary as they come; middle-aged, slightly furtive, as though bracing him-self for a kick in the rump. The 'Chopper' was a relic from his Borstal days when he was alleged to have the best-developed virile attachments of his entry – not that they had ever done him any good, because no woman ever stayed with him long.

In his younger days he had done a bit of front porch stuff, nothing ambitious or too nervy: in and out quickly with whatever he could grab. He had a record that should have depressed him if he ever examined it honestly, which he never did. He had done clerical work for long-term mail order frauds, and he had been the unlucky one who stayed too late and got caught.

The back seat contents of parked cars were his current interest; it was hard work and demanded a lot of mileage out of a bloke, nipping around where those bloody wardens didn't happen to be, in the better shopping areas.

Now Sam was remembering how smart Chopper was with most kinds of locks, and not only on cars. He ordered two whiskies. They exchanged the accepted lies about how well each was doing, and so forth.

Two drinks later, paid for by Sam because Chopper had discovered that he had come out without his wallet, and Sam began to move in on what he had in mind.

'Do me a favour, Chopper,' he said. 'I had to ditch my car outside my place in Porchester Walk not more than twenty minutes back, left the keys in it and all ... there was this bloke, see, breathing down my neck and I reckoned I'd better take off quick like ... to tell you the truth I been giving his bird the old treatment and he found out ... now I need that car – it's worth a couple of quid.'

Chopper held out his hand, under the edge of the bar.

He couldn't take a light for his cigarette without making it look like a conspiracy. Sam slid him two folded notes.

'I'll be looking for you outside Lancaster tube station,' he said. 'Play it nice and cool, Chopper ... there might be a little piece of business we might share ... later, see what I mean?'

Chopper gave him a disbelieving stare, because Sam had a lousy reputation for leaving a partner with the dirty end of the stick.

'Straight up,' said Sam.

Chopper finished his drink, he knew another wasn't coming his way. 'See you,' he said, and drifted out, leaving Sam with the uneasy feeling that perhaps he'd been had for a mug after all – Chopper might just evaporate, with a couple of quid of Sam's money.

He did Chopper an injustice. In less than half an hour, Chopper slid up to the kerb where Sam waited. Sam got in beside him and told him to turn into the park, then right and up by the Serpentine. They parked under the shade of the trees.

'Some bleeder nicked the keys and left it locked,' said Chopper. 'Lucky for you I had mine with me.' Chopper habitually carried keys to fit most standard makes.

'No trouble otherwise?' said Sam.

'Wasn't around there long enough to see,' said Chopper. 'Soon as I got in I come out in reverse ... I didn't see nobody.'

Boats were being heaved about on the shining water by sweaty citizens, with their birds trailing their pinkies over the side. Sun-bathers baked themselves. The exhibitionists strutted about and flexed their muscles. Some even went swimming.

It was hot inside the car, and Chopper didn't smell very fragrant around the feet. So Sam got out and sat on the dusty grass. Chopper joined him.

'You said you got something else, Sam.'

'Could be,' said Sam. 'You interested then?'

Chopper shrugged. 'How much?'

Sam made a disgusted sound. 'That's the wrong attitude, Chopper ... you know I'd give you a fair crack of the whip ... but if you got something better to do don't let me stand in your way.'

The mean bastard, thought Chopper. All big talk, that was Sam Harris.

'I didn't mean it like that, Sammie.'

'Suit yourself,' said Sam nonchalantly. 'It might have been worth five ones to do something that won't take you five minutes, a smart bloke like you.'

'So what do I have to do?' said Chopper cautiously. Sam Harris wasn't any fairy godmother.

'Listen,' said San, 'there's this empty flat, the bird who lives there is a very good friend of mine, as a matter of fact I was with her there last night – you getting the picture, Chopper? She's a high-class bird, and she don't like no scandal, see what I mean?'

Chopper didn't, but he nodded.

'To cut a long story short,' said Sam, 'I left my case there last night, black leather job, in the cabinet just inside her hall ... and now I need it back. It's got some business papers, confidential stuff ... the point is that I can't take the risk of being seen inside the building in daylight – there's another bloke reckons he's got a prior claim, and he doesn't go much on me ... that's why I had to ditch the car.'

Chopper didn't believe a word of it. 'You get about, don't you?' he said. 'Proper Lover-Boy. What happens when this bloke sees me at the flat? Am I supposed to be invisible? Or don't it matter if I get clobbered on account of a bird I've never even seen?'

'He doesn't know you,' said Sam patiently. 'If he's there he'll be watching the main entrance – I'll show you the side entrance through some shops. Her flat is on the second landing, right opposite the lifts. Yale lock.'

'And you say the place is empty?'

'Just to make sure I'll ring, and you can listen for yourself.'

'Been a long time since I did anything in that line,' said Chopper, but he was weakening.

'In and out, nothing to it,' said Sam. 'Five quid when I get that case in my hands. If you don't fancy it, I'll look around. I got another bloke in mind.' Sam got to his feet and dusted the grass off his trousers.

'Yale lock?' said Chopper.

'You'll laugh at it,' said Sam, 'bloke with your skill. Are you on? Don't let me talk you into it… I just thought you could use a little loose change.'

Chopper stood up. 'You drive me over there,' he said. 'I'll take a look at it first.'

'Why not?' said Sam. 'It'll be the softest five you ever picked up.'

They got into the car, Chopper wanted to know what this other bloke looked like, and Sam gave him a fanciful description – over six foot tall, with a black beard.

'Ugly great bastard,' said Sam. 'You couldn't miss him if he's about.'

When they got near the building, Sam stopped at a phone booth, and they both crammed into it. Sam found Myra's address, pointed it out to Chopper, with the number.

'Try it yourself,' he said. 'She's out.'

Chopper dialled, and got nothing but the *burr-burr.* He began to look a little less doubtful.

'See what I mean?' said Sam. 'Nothing to it.'

He showed Chopper the arcade entrance at the side. 'The black case in the hall cupboard, Chopper, that's all, you get me?'

Chopper pursed his lips and dragged down the corners of his mouth. 'You asking me or telling me?'

'She'd miss anything else,' said Sam. 'She'd make a stink … might be awkward for me…'

'You carrying her insurance?' said Chopper. 'You won't lose nothing.' He squinted up at the building in the bright afternoon sun. Anybody who could live there had stuff worth bothering about, and Chopper didn't include a black leather case.

'I'll see what I feel about it,' said Chopper, 'once I get inside.' He was the boss. 'If you don't trust me you'd better come with me.'

Sam patted his shoulder. 'I just don't want you to spoil it, Chopper.'

'I won't,' said Chopper. 'Where will you be?'

'At the bottom end, just this side of the corner,' said Sam. 'Use the arcade entrance both ways.'

'Ten minutes,' said Chopper and got out of the car.

Sam drove some thirty yards down and parked. He lit a cigarette to show himself that there was nothing to worry about. Chopper was as dumb as they make them, but he could fiddle a lock. He would certainly help himself to any small items that took his fancy, and Sam would prise them off him later. He could handle Chopper.

After six minutes he decided to do a discreet circle of the building, see what might be around the main entrance, any sign of that black Mercedes parked on the drive-in, like last night.

Bonner lived there, if he had told Chopper that – Chopper wouldn't have fallen for it.

He drove down to the corner, turned right and then right again to cruise up past the front entrance. And it was then that he caught sight of something that he couldn't believe – Chopper nipping across the road at the top, with that case, Chopper certainly not making for the rendezvous.

The nerve of the little git, trying that on Sam Harris. As Sam accelerated, a taxi did a crazy U-turn right in front of him, and then by the time he was clear, Chopper had rounded the top corner and was into the main road, where he could lose himself in the traffic, hop on a bus.

Sam hadn't felt so savage and affronted for a long time. You just couldn't trust anybody. Chopper Roberts, of all people.

Sam swung into the main road. A bus was

pulling away from a stop, and he saw the back view of Chopper on the platform – the coloured conductor was wagging a finger and saying something, and Chopper went aloft.

San drove slowly behind the bus. The one thing he had to watch for was if the bus stopped right beside a tube station and Chopper did a quick transfer down below, he might lose him then. And he wasn't going to do that. The bus trundled on, it was the slack period in the middle of the after-noon. If he had to pass the bus Chopper would see him. So he would let the bus stay there in front.

It took a bit of juggling, with cars and vans parked near the bus stops, but he managed it, and got himself soundly cursed by drivers behind who couldn't see why the hell he was dawdling. Chopper didn't come down at any of the stops, and one of them was right alongside a tube station.

On a clear stretch of road, Sam got an idea. The bus was slowing at a stop where nobody waited, and an elderly lady was being helped to the platform by the con-ductor.

Sam stopped right there behind the bus, taking his ignition key, the spare one donated by Chopper himself. And when the elderly lady was finally clear of the platform and on the pavement, Sam boarded the bus and went to the upper deck.

There were a few passengers, and Chopper was right up in the front seat, alone, and as Sam approached he saw the case balanced on Chopper's lap, Chopper's arms wrapped around it.

Sam took the empty seat. Chopper looked at him, swallowed.

'Well, Chopper,' said Sam softly. 'I see you got it.' And he removed the case from Chopper's nerveless grip.

'Listen, Sam,' said Chopper.

Sam nodded, got up and made his way back and down. The conductor looked at him. 'Sorry,' said Sam, 'wrong bus, I'm getting off next stop.'

Chopper came down, looking like a man who has made up his mind to face the worst. He glanced at Sam and Sam ignored him, waiting for the bus to stop, the case tucked underneath his arm. The bus stopped and they both got off. Sam started back to where he had left his car, and Chopper followed. Sam didn't look at him or speak to him, just walked on briskly.

'Sammie,' said Chopper tentatively, 'you

owe me five.'

'Little twister,' said Sam, quite pleasantly. 'Beat it.'

'You owe me five – you got what you wanted.'

'I owe you nothing,' said Sam.

'You got it all wrong,' said Chopper. 'I wasn't trying to run out on you, honest–'

Sam laughed. 'Do me a favour – just push off before I tread you into the pavement.' He was moving so briskly now that Chopper had almost to trot to keep up with him.

'Sammie – you don't think I'd try any funny stuff with you, do you? You know me, I wouldn't try anything like that… I got the case didn't I? And it wasn't where you said it was, I had to search for it … and if you want to know what I think, I don't think it's your case–'

'Where was it?'

'Top of the wardrobe in her bedroom,' said Chopper. 'Where they always hide things.'

Sam halted. 'That a fact?'

'In the bedroom,' said Chopper. 'There was nothing in that cupboard but junk … so I hadda do one of the quickest rummages you ever saw … she got some nice gear up there, but I never touched any of it.'

He held his arms clear of his body, inviting Sam to investigate. 'I reckon you owe me something, Sam–'

Sam had started walking again. 'It beats me how you got the face to tag along after what you tried to do,' he said.

'There was this big feller with the black beard, like you told me,' said Chopper. 'He was there hanging around, and I hadda give him the slip – I reckon he had his eye on me as I come down them stairs, proper great bastard … so I ducked out the front way, there wasn't anything else I could do–'

'–And you were going to get in touch with me later and hand over the case.' Sam was smiling, not a nice smile.

'That's right,' said Chopper, hopefully. 'Most blokes would have got into a panic–'

'–But not you,' said Sam.

'I always use my loaf,' said Chopper. 'So how about that five, Sammie? I know that case don't belong to you–'

'No? What makes you so sure?'

Chopper gave a knowing grin. 'You never owned one like that, so don't give me any more of that crap. That's real leather.'

'You're a proper little twister,' said Sam. 'I wonder what made you think you could act funny with me?'

'I told you,' said Chopper. 'I hadda dodge this feller—'

'There wasn't any big bloke with a black beard,' said Sam. 'I just made him up, which makes you a lying bastard... You'll get nothing from me except maybe a swift kick in the crotch.'

Chopper whispered something inaudible. Then: 'Okay, boyo, you're the smart one ... so what's in the case?'

'Listen, Chopper, I've had my fill of you – you tried to pull a fast one and it came unstuck ... now beat it, you hear me?'

Chopper heard all right, but he kept on padding alongside. 'You got the case,' he said. 'It ain't yours, and I want to see what's inside ... you didn't even know where it was.'

They reached Sam's car. 'Push off,' said Sam.

Chopper slid into the passenger seat. 'I reckon I got a stake in this business,' he said. 'Let's see what's in the case, Sammie.'

Sam got behind the wheel; the case was on his lap and would get in the way when he drove. But he wasn't going to let Chopper handle it at this stage. He tucked it between his seat and the door. And glared across at Chopper.

81

'I wouldn't try anything rough if I was you,' said Chopper, 'and you don't scare me, Sammie–'

'I'd like to twist your neck,' said Sam. He started the car and drove carefully away. He was trying to think how he could get rid of this nosy little shyster.

Porchester Walk was out, there would be somebody watching. Myra must have seen the case – nobody else could have moved it into her bedroom. It wasn't proving as simple as he hoped – he'd have to shed Chopper and without any fuss.

Chopper laughed.

'What's funny?' said Sam.

'I was just thinking,' said Chopper. 'You say there wasn't any big feller with a black beard – but there was a bloke looked like that waiting outside that flower shop when I come out. Where we going, Sammie?'

'I need a drink,' said Sam. 'Then we can talk business, I know a place in Notting Hill … maybe you'll get your five quid after all.'

Chopper liked the sound of that. The 'Blue Heaven' had little to offer at that hour of the afternoon except inferior drinks at inflated prices. At the far end of the main room there was a tiny stage where nightly 'performances' happened, mostly in drag, that being the current vogue.

There was one tired lady available, but Sam told her to take off and he didn't mean her tatty gown. He had brought the case in with him and it sat in his lap.

Chopper drank two large pseudo-Scotches in rapid style. Presently he had to excuse himself to attend to his bladder. Sam directed him – along the back stairs and up to the next floor...

When Chopper returned there was of course no Sam Harris, and Sam hadn't even had the decency to settle the chit for the drinks. And that was in brief the pattern of Chopper's life. No luck at all.

FIVE

Aristide Apian had listened to Ric Bonner's report with a faintly weary expression on his face.

'This is a great nonsense,' he said. 'I would say you have made every possible mistake. If this man is nothing of importance then why did he go to such trouble to avoid you? To make you appear so stupid?'

'He knew the district, I didn't,' said Bonner. 'I was unlucky.'

'Consider the position,' said Apian. 'We have a man about whom we know nothing – I would say he is a professional with plenty of nerve.'

Bonner shook his head. 'You should have seen him last night, he's no professional, Sophie tossed him about and he was scared–'

'–My dear Bonner,' said Apian, 'that only proves my point, he put on a performance last night, he fooled all of you – he is clearly a man of resource ... now where is he?'

Bonner shrugged. It was useless to argue with Apian.

'Go back to the flat and clear out your safe,' said Apian. 'You will keep nothing that might interest other people.'

'There isn't anything,' said Bonner sourly. 'Voyses took what mattered–'

'–And now this unknown man has it,' said Apian. 'Have you thought what this means?'

'We'll have to make some adjustments.'

Apian laughed silently. 'So all our preparations are to go for nothing because you allow a stranger to make rings round you? If my name were Yassir Arafat you would not be making any more mistakes – he would eliminate you without a second thought. I am giving you another chance … and Lockerton Camp still remains our objective. You will arrange to see the others immediately, you will tell them nothing of what has happened, but they are to find other lodgings right away – tell them it is our normal precaution.'

'Timmins won't like that,' said Bonner. 'He's jittery enough as it is.'

'Fifty pounds will soothe his nerves, we can't replace him at this stage.'

'I'll need some money for the others,' said Bonner. 'They were bleating about it the last time we met.'

Apian got up and went over to the safe set

in the wall of the room, and he carefully shielded the face of the safe so that Bonner couldn't follow his movements and guess at the combination. Nobody but Apian had access to the safe or knew just how much it held.

Over his shoulder he said, 'This has been an expensive error on your part, I do dislike the thought of our funds being in the wrong hands... Voyses at least was in the business and knew the risks he ran.'

'Didn't do him much good in the end,' said Bonner.

'He should not have been allowed to die like that, it was profitless, and I do not like waste.'

'Take it up with Rass,' said Bonner. 'He's your hatchet man.'

'I have,' said Apian. 'I have sent him back, and he will be found more suitable employment in Paris or Marseilles, where they are not so squeamish – Voyses was a great disappointment to him.'

Apian brought over three neat piles of five pound notes, pulled out a drawer in his desk and took out three long envelopes. Smiling at Bonner, he slipped the notes into the envelopes and sealed them. Then slid them across the desk.

'Fifty each, deal first with Timmins and make sure you quieten him down. Tell him you need another plan of the Camp by tomorrow – and this time bring it to me here.'

Bonner slipped the envelopes into his pockets and stood up. 'It won't go astray,' he said.

'The other one did,' said Apian. 'Tomorrow you will go down to Lockerton and take a long look around – we must know if there have been any new precautions, and sudden changes, you know what to look for – take Timmins with you.'

'I know what to do,' said Bonner. 'I don't need Timmins.'

'After last night,' said Apian pleasantly, 'you need all the help you can get.'

On the way downstairs Bonner met Sophie coming up, in a fetching outfit he had never seen her wearing before, and he knew her wardrobe intimately. She smiled, quite unabashed, and gave him the bedroom look he knew so well also. On the sunlit landing there in front of the window she posed.

'How do I look, Ric? Like it?'

'Bitch,' he said and went on down.

'And the best of luck to you as well,' she called after him. If she had to sleep with

Apian she might as well get the rate for the job, and a girl could always use new clothes.

From a phone box in Hammersmith, Bonner made his calls. Timmins first because he mattered most. Timmins was in. They were to meet outside the Star And Garter entrance to Richmond park at five thirty, Timmins was to pack a case and say he was going to be away on business.

'Panic?' said Timmins.

'Not a bit of it,' said Bonner. 'Play it cool.'

'You know me,' said Timmins.

'Be there,' said Bonner.

Promptly on the half hour Henry Timmins came up Richmond Hill, in his Viva, looking like what he now was, a travelling rep, except that the case on the back seat held no samples. Thirty-six years old, Timmins was smart in appearance, with plenty of the military style still about him – a tidy moustache, short hair, and a brisk manner, not quite officer material, though he liked to give the impression that he had in fact held a commission.

At the time of the Court Martial that had terminated his connection with Her Majesty's Service he had been a Sergeant with plenty of seniority. Technically he had been thought a good soldier by his superiors, until they had stumbled on his weakness of confusing Government property and cash with his own, to the expense of the public purse. He had been doing it for years overseas, but a home posting had been his undoing, and he had become careless, and the chopper had fallen.

He had salted a bit away, so when he came out of the glasshouse and found his wife had moved on he was not unduly disturbed. There was no great rush to engage his services, most civilian employers being coy about a Court Martial subject, and he spent some months in enforced idleness, which had dented his capital.

Eventually he got himself a job with a firm of fancy goods and toy manufacturers, selling on commission plus modest expenses. He made a living.

Bonner was in the white Mini that he used when contacting Timmins and the others; there were thousands like it, and the number plates were never as readable as they should be.

Timmins followed Bonner into the park. Timmins would have preferred a pub, but Bonner had this thing about meeting in the open air. Proper cloak and dagger stuff.

Some few years earlier, Timmins and Bonner had served on the same camp, but then it had been Captain Richard Bonner, and a right toffee-nosed bastard he had been. It was different now, they were level, and Timmins didn't have to call him Sir – a cashiered officer didn't rate any more than a former N.C.O. – Bonner had got himself into a bad tangle over Mess Funds, and officers and gentlemen weren't supposed to do that.

They parked the cars and walked over to a seat under the trees, not looking like friends.

'How soon can you do me another map of Lockerton?' said Bonner.

'What happened to the other?' said Timmins. 'Wasn't it good enough?'

'I need another, by tomorrow.' Bonner took out an envelope and put it on the seat between them. 'Fifty,' he said.

Timmins took the envelope and slipped it into his jacket pocket. 'Can do. Where will I see you?'

'Where will you be tonight?'

'I know a place at Staines,' said Timmins. 'I'll be okay–'

'–I wasn't worrying about your comfort,' said Bonner, a little frostily. He sounded just like a bleeding officer, Timmins reflected.

'I'll pick you up at Staines station at two tomorrow afternoon,' said Bonner. 'We're going down to Lockerton.'

'Anything special come up?' said Timmins. 'I was there last week.'

'We need another recce – that's all.'

'That'll be Friday,' said Timmins. 'Slack afternoon down there, blokes bogging off early for a crafty week-end, not many about.'

'Exactly,' said Bonner, and got up. He walked off without saying farewell. He never did. Timmins sat for a minute and thought about the girl he used to fancy down at Staines. A couple of gins at the Packhorse and he'd be there, boy. Just like Mister Bloody ex-Captain Bonner not to explain why he had to change billets in such a hurry.

Still, fifty nicker was better than a slap in the belly. And five hundred to come. Maybe a bit more if it all went off right, so Bonner said and it wasn't his money he was giving out. Bloody wogs must have money to burn, and what a right cock-up they made of anything they tried on their own. Proper pathetic.

In a fairly buoyant mood, Timmins strolled across and got into his car and by that time Bonner was out of sight – you'd think the whole of Scotland Yard was out looking for him. Timmins drove out of the park and down to 'The Lass of Richmond Hill' where he bought himself two quick pints just to get the taste. Nobody about yet. Too early. But he wasn't going to be drinking on his own later.

Bonner had two more calls to make. Fenna came next, he should be home by now – he was supposed to keep himself handy to a phone each evening between six and eight in case Bonner wanted him. Fenna's mother answered and said her son was having his tea; she went to fetch him. She was a widow and Ted Fenna was her only child, and she liked to know what he was up to. Some hopes. But at least Bonner's voice sounded gentlemanly. She would have been worried if it had been a call from a girl. One of those nasty bits with nothing but sex on her mind, but her Ted wasn't like that, he was a good boy.

Ted Fenna was twenty-nine; he worked in the transport section of a factory on the Great West Road, where he was known as a skilled mechanic with a touch of genius in the way he could handle most kinds of engines; not a good mixer with his mates, he was reckoned to be a bit of a commie, and best left on his own. Tall and scrawny, he wore his dark hair long, and dressed pretty sharply in the evenings and at week-ends.

He didn't have much to do with girls, and he wasn't the other sort either. He was just Ted Fenna who preferred his own company, most of the time. He had a secondhand Sprite that he had picked up cheap and had worked on until it was better than the makers would ever have claimed for a new model. His private dream was an Aston-Martin, and a trip right through the middle of Europe and down to Italy where they had some real roads.

When Bonner parked outside the walled yard and let himself into the warehouse, he found Fenna in overalls already at work on the canvas-backed truck, finishing off the Wessex Div insignia on the wing and tail-board.

Fenna nodded at him and went on working, he handled a paint brush as neatly and as efficiently as he handled a spanner on the innards of an engine in trouble. Bonner lit a cigarette and went over to inspect the Humber staff car. He walked around it and he couldn't fault it. It would pass anywhere. The right markings. With a driver in uniform and an officer in the back, no sentry on a gate was going to do anything but give it a smart salute. And the truck would trundle in behind.

Ted Fenna had found both the Humber and the truck – ex-Army surplus, cheap and no questions asked. They had needed working on, and Fenna had worked on them alone in the warehouse, for an extra thirty quid a week, and he didn't have to be told what they were for. He knew where to find things – a gear-box for an Opel Kapitan 1939, for instance, or a steering column for an obsolete M.G. model, and nobody in the breakdown trade ever diddled him.

One day he would run his own outfit, assembling and fitting and tuning vintage jobs. There was big money in it if you knew your way around.

'The Humber looks good,' said Bonner.

'Should do,' said Fenna. 'Spent enough time on it. What's this lark about telling me to move out for a bit? Running into some trouble?'

'We're too careful for that,' said Bonner casually. 'It's just a little precaution, if you like. You haven't been getting any strange phone calls at home, have you? Calls from people you don't know?'

Fenna cleared a space for himself on the littered worktable, and sat. 'Somebody been showing an interest in us, that what you mean?'

He didn't sound scared. For the money he was getting, and for what he was going to do, there had to be some kind of risk. Like driving fast in bad road conditions. In Ted Fenna's make-up there were many of the qualities of nerve and drive that take some men to the top. Or to jail.

'No panic,' said Bonner. He took out the envelope and passed it to Fenna. 'That should cover any extra expenses for a few nights. What did you tell your old lady?'

'She thinks the firm is sending me up to Brum. I been up there before. She's okay, and I know of some digs in West Drayton, but I'll be here most nights. How much longer you reckon we got?'

'Maybe a week.'

'Then I reckon I'd better get a move on,' said Fenna, getting briskly off the table. 'The brakes on the truck aren't all that good, and the steering's still ropy. She'll need a bloody good road test, and I can't do that around here except at night.'

'Aim for the end of next week,' said Bonner. 'Everything all right otherwise? I like your paint-work, looks good.'

Before Bonner left the warehouse, Fenna was already back at work, the industrious craftsman. As soon as he heard Bonner's car leaving, he took out the envelope and checked the money. Fifty, in fives. More than he had expected. The digs in West Drayton wouldn't come to more than fifteen and six bed and breakfast. Dinner in the works canteen, a couple of bob. So he'd be saving most of that fifty. Plus thirty for another week on the night work. And the big dollop yet to come. That Aston-Martin might be nearer than he thought.

Bonner's last call that night was at a large block of flats in Maida Vale, near Warwick Avenue, one of those slab-sided blocks that fail to be fashionable and yet remain much too expensive. He went up in the lift to the floor next to the top where the flats were the smallest and cheapest – little more than bed-sitters with tiny kitchen alcoves and microscopic bathrooms.

Tessie Raikes was in the late thirties, but not wearing too well. She had always been a fine figure of a woman, with statuesque thighs and abundant breasts, and a surprisingly trim waist. A good sport, ready to stand her round at the bar and swap dirty stories with the best of them. Plenty of gusto and ready for most emergencies, that was Tessie. You knew where you were with her – healthy and uncomplicated, and if you wanted to take her to bed she rarely disappointed.

She had seen service in the WRAC as a driver, the life had suited her, and she might have made something of a career at it if she hadn't written-off a staff car one night when loaded with gin and hampered by the amorous attentions of a civilian passenger, male and just as sloshed as Tessie. Two in the morning is no time to wreck the Brigadier's favourite car, especially when you have no authority to be driving it.

Since then Tessie had followed a variety of occupations, but none of them for long. She had served behind a number of bars but she liked the stuff too much herself, and her reckonings were likely to be sketchy as the evening wore on. She had done bits of crowd work in films of no importance, and she had even appeared in a brief television series that attracted no kind of attention. On the strength of this she thought of herself as an actress, 'resting', and she had been 'resting' now for six solid years.

She could type and take shorthand, she could also wait at table – but not for long.

She needed a nice sensible husband, and a couple of strapping kids, and she had none of these. The trim waist was thickening, but her legs were still good, and there was nothing wrong with her digestion. A good skin and a head of real blonde hair.

In a skimpy pale blue wrap, her feet bare and her hair free to brush her shoulders, she opened the door to Bonner and gave him the widest of wide smiles, as though he must be the only man she ever wanted to see.

'Ric,' she said warmly, 'come on in, do – excuse me, but I've just got out of the bath … how nice to see you again.'

He followed her in and he knew there was nothing under that wrap but Tessie, lots of Tessie.

'I can't stop long,' he said.

'Don't be like that,' said Tessie. 'What'll you have? There's gin or vodka … or a teeny drop of whisky that I've been saving specially for you.'

'Whisky,' he said to avoid one of the wrangles she made such a thing of. He wrinkled his nose at the overpowering feminine scent of the room. Tessie always overdid it.

She gave him the whisky and it wasn't so teeny. She had vodka and lime, and he knew it wasn't her first that evening. She arranged herself on the chesterfield so that the shaded light was on her legs which that wrap did little to conceal. Tessie was always trying. She was attractive, if you liked them big all round. He thought of Sophie and Apian, and the way Sophie had looked in that new gear – at least with Tessie there would be no strings attached.

He took out the envelope and tossed it into her lap.

'Fifty,' he said, 'as I told you over the phone, I want you to change your address for a little while.'

'Anything you say. Trouble, Ric?'

'No,' he said. 'Just playing it safe.'

'I'm packed and ready,' she said. 'They're keeping a room for me in Leinster Gardens … a double room.'

He knew she was smiling, her face was in shadow. 'I'll drive you,' he said.

'Nice man. We don't have to hurry, do we? You've got something on your mind, Ric, I can tell … is everything going all right?'

He nodded.

'I'm glad you called,' she said. 'It's been a lousy week. It's nice to see a friendly face for a change. How's young Fenna getting on with the vehicles?'

'Nearly ready,' said Bonner. 'We might be on the move next week-end.'

'It can't come too soon for me,' said Tessie. 'I hate this hanging around. Know what I'm going to do when it's all over? I'm going to buy myself a month or so in Majorca, in the sun, with people having some fun ... would you come over and see me, Ric?'

'I might do that,' he said.

She uncoiled herself and poured him another drink. All he had to do was to reach out and there she was.

'Well I've heard a man sound more enthusiastic,' she said lightly. 'I can't even give it away, can I?'

'You're fine.' He ran the back of his hand down her thigh.

She paused for a moment, looking down at him, her full lower lip thrust out, perhaps smiling. Then she walked into the bedroom next door, leaving the door open. He sat with his drink. It would be the first time – so what the hell. He looked at his watch. Not yet ten o'clock. He'd been on the go since early that morning and most of the night before.

He could hear her moving about in there, then the creak of the bed. He finished the whisky and walked into the bedroom. Tessie sat on the edge of the bed, without her wrap, leaning back on her arms.

'What kept you?' she said. 'Come to mamma.'

He closed the door behind him, and Tessie swung her legs up onto the bed. No fuss.

SIX

Sam found a quiet side street. He had to use the pliers and the screwdriver from his tool-kit before he got that case undone, and he ruined both locks in the process.

Inside there was a folder with papers, typewritten sheets, and what looked like some maps or diagrams; not very interesting, he thought. But there was another large fat envelope, sealed and with no address. He slit it open and took out a sealed packet; there was name typed on it – *Henry Timmins*, and in the top right hand corner where a stamp might have been there was the figure 500. Inside the packet he found a tight wedge of fivers, all new.

Carefully keeping his hands out of sight in the car, Sam extracted a note and looked at it, unable to believe his luck. It was the kind of thing you dream of – they weren't bouncers, they weren't sludge, they were real! He took out four more notes and they felt beautiful, just beautiful – crisp and tidy. He folded them away into his wallet.

There were two more packets, of the same size. One with the name of *Tessie Raikes* typed, the other *Edward Fenna;* both carried the number 500. They were sealed and he didn't open them.

He sat back and thought about having fifteen hundred quid in his lap like that. Fantastic. No wonder that mob had been leaping around. Fifteen hundred! Sam couldn't remember when he'd had a nicer tickle. Nothing to flog. All ready for spending. It made him sweat and he tried to light a cigarette without knowing what he was doing.

He stowed the case out of sight under the passenger's seat, and it was some minutes before he felt ready to drive. Chopper Robins would cry for a month if he knew what he had missed, and he had damn nearly got it.

Sam drove around until he found the shops he needed. He bought a case with a good lock, two shirts, pyjamas, socks and shaving gear, enough for a start. Later on he could spread himself at his leisure, fit himself out properly. Take a nice long holiday. Brighton maybe, you could always find action there if you had money to toss around. Dollies. Rich mugs. Sharp boys who weren't as sharp as they thought. This was going to be a good summer, all the signs were there – wonderful what a difference a bit of cash made, say fifteen hundred dropping out of the blue when you needed it.

Sam's first impulse was to take a quick sniff around the West End, the spots he knew best; but caution sent him out on to the Portsmouth Road, and he booked into a goodish hotel near Esher, a place with some class where they wouldn't go through his luggage.

Up in his room, with a large whisky brought up to him he had a happy count and verified that each of those packets had contained five hundred in fives – he spread them out on his bed, and he had never seen a sweeter sight. All profit. No wonder that Sophie bird and that bastard Bonner had been steamed up. Little Sammie had diddled them all. He wouldn't move around with less than fifty in his wallet. It was like being a foot taller.

He stacked the money and locked it away, then lay on his bed and looked at the folder. There were some sheets of what looked like notes about a military camp, and one of the diagrams was of a camp, showing roads and buildings.

Outside the main guard-room there was a

road, marked to Lockerton village. There was an officers' mess, and a sergeants' mess, a parade ground right in the middle of a mess of buildings, surrounded by barrack blocks.

Standing on its own at the top of the sketch, and near the sports field, there was a building that had been ringed in pencil – the armoury; in the margin there was a pencilled annotation: Sgt. Martin i/c. Cpls. Willis and Carter.

Sam's interest grew. Somebody had gone to a lot of trouble getting this stuff together.

Part of one sheet had details about the Commanding Officer's weekly parade, which took place on Saturday mornings, apparently, three Saturdays out of four.

The parade marched on at 0830 hrs. Inspection by Company Commanders. Colour Hoist and March Past. Parade march off 0945 hrs. Barrack room inspection: 1000 hrs – 1100 hours. Coaches depart Main Guard-Room 1200 hrs.

The Commanding Officer, Lt.-Col. E.J.C. Bamford, D.S.O. Adjutant Capt. H. Crewe. Armament officer – Lieut. P. Dunne. Officers mess sherry party, 1215 hrs – 1300 hrs … all officers on camp attend.

Dunne on Command cricket team – this

sentence was underlined, with an extra note: check fixture list. Timmins to arrange. Also week-end Duty Officer roster for next two weeks. Check manning of north gate.

Another underlined sentence ran: *Duty officer checks Armoury and Range, 1530 hrs. – 1545 hrs., duty armourer reports and stands by. Armoury windows and entrances visible only from front of Gymnasium which should not be in use week-ends. Check no field exercises for week-end 18. Timmins to clear with Halley.*

Consider possibility of exit by north gate if open and manned.

Sam's connection with the armed forces had been brief and inglorious, much of it spent in detention or on extra fatigues, but he didn't need to be a Field Marshal Lord Montgomery to realise what he had just been looking at. Somebody had been doing a lot of research on this camp, and the objective was clearly the armoury. This was Thursday, the 9th, so the week-end of the 18th would be next but one … and then something out of the ordinary was planned to happen at this Lockerton place.

Military camps had been broken into before … by some of the Irish lads, and the Welsh nationalist boyos, and guns and so forth had been nicked. Sam had read about them, and he wondered which lot these were. He had no special feelings either way. Live and let live. At least he had lifted some of their cash. Which put him one up, didn't it?

It was against all of Sam's principles to contact the police on a thing like this; the less he had to do with the fuzz the happier he was likely to be; they'd only lean on him and put him through the mangle and make a mess of his life, they might even find out about the money, they were such persistent bastards ... they'd have him tied up in it somehow, asking all kinds of awkward questions.

He had the three names: Tessie Raikes, Edward Fenna, and Henry Timmins. He could start with them. Throw a bit of a scare into them – there might be more money to be picked up. This wasn't a legit operation ... and look at the way they had chased after the case.

A little pressure now to start them sweating. He locked the papers away with the money and went down to the phones by the dining-room. He found a number for Edward Fenna, first, so he dialled it. A woman answered.

'Is Mr Edward Fenna there?' said Sam.

'Not back from the factory yet,' said the woman in an elderly glum voice. 'Who shall I say called?'

'Never mind,' said Sam. 'I'll try again later.'

There was no phone listed for Henry Timmins, but there was one for Tessie Raikes. He tried her, although he would have preferred a man because you could never tell how a woman was going to react, and he was sure she wouldn't be one of the bosses – if they were aiming to bust into an army camp they wouldn't use women. Anyway, the problem didn't arise because there wasn't any answer.

He made a note of the Fenna address and went into the bar, at peace with the world. Then he ate his way through a good menu, with armagnac and a cigar, and tipped the waiter heavily to ensure the best attention for the rest of his visit. It was a couple of hours later before he tried the Fenna number again, the old lady told him her son had been sent up to Birmingham by his firm and she didn't know where he would be staying.

Sam thought that had a bit of a smell about it. 'When do you expect him back?' he asked.

'Next week, he don't tell me much, I'm only his old mother...' Sam put the phone down while she was still rabbiting on about her son.

He thought about Tessie Raikes, and decided to make it personal. So he got out his car and drove back into London. He was just pulling up outside the block in Maida Vale when he saw Ric Bonner cross the pavement, in company with a well-built woman with nice legs; they looked very chummy and got into a white Mini, and Bonner was carrying a case; the bird wasn't Sophie, too big and too old.

They took off at speed, and Sam was caught facing the wrong way, so that by the time he had jockeyed himself around he had lost them. Sam wasn't any middle-of-the-road creeper, he liked to belt along, but that Mini had gone like a bomb. Hell. He was sure they hadn't seen him.

Gerald Payne, nineteen, a second year engineering student at Kingston poly, had borrowed his father's car for the evening. It was a Rover 2000, newish, and his old man had warned him to do nothing daft, like wrapping it around a lamp post. The prohibition hadn't included the carriage of passengers, such as Marilyn – blonde, eighteen and a bit over, ready to live for ever and make love whenever possible; a dolly with talent and enthusiasm.

They drove down the lane by Thorpe and stopped by the gate. 'Okay?' said Gerald.

Marilyn glanced at the bracken, and then at Gerald, and she was smiling, her womanly grown-up smile, showing the tip of a pink tongue.

They got out and Gerald pushed the gate open. Arms entwined, they made for the bracken, where there was a path of sorts. It was beautifully quiet and empty.

In a matter of seconds they were back, Marilyn first, stumbling and white, to lean on the gate with her shoulders heaving and her face hidden on her arms.

'I'm going to be sick,' she whispered. Gerald held her but she wasn't sick. Just scared. 'He was dead wasn't he?'

Gerald helped her into the car, and he wasn't feeling too special himself. He had never seen a dead body before.

'We'll have to tell somebody,' he said. 'We can't just leave it...'

'Must we...? I want to go home, Gerry...'

'We'll have to tell the police,' he said stubbornly. 'Then I'll take you home.'

Some hours later that night, Inspector Charles Morton, of the Special Branch, on night duty at the Yard, was studying the telex report in company with his Sergeant, Walter Pritchard; Morton was young for his rank, being little more than thirty, which meant that he had to be good, and he was. Pritchard was five years older, a little too plump, but reliable, and possessed of a photographic memory.

The body of a middle-aged man, so far not identified, found in a Surrey copse ... severe burn marks on the soles of both feet and on the lower belly. No other marks of violence. The preliminary medical report placed death within the last forty-eight hours. There would be an autopsy in the morning...

'He was wearing shoes and socks,' said Morton. 'Put on after death. Why burn his feet? To loosen his tongue? I wonder if he talked?'

Sergeant Pritchard, who was loaded with odd bits of erudition, said, 'That's an old bandit custom, chief. Corsica, Sicily, round there. That's how we got the word "chauffeur" – foot-warmer. That's how they used to coax travellers to divulge where they'd

111

hidden their gold. Very historical.'

'Thanks a lot,' said Morton. 'Very inform-ative.'

'It doesn't happen too often over here,' said Pritchard. 'We're civilised.'

'I hadn't noticed,' said Morton. 'So you see a touch of the mysterious Orient here, do you? On the strength of a corpse with singed feet?'

'Mediterranean isn't the Orient, chief.'

'You're very sharp tonight,' said Morton.

'It might be something in our line,' said Pritchard. 'No harm in looking. Like me to go?'

'We'll both go.' Morton reached for the phone to clear their passage; at this stage this was a C.I.D. enquiry, and identification was the first priority. If the Special Branch thought they could help they would be welcome, and so forth. Half an hour later they were driving down to Surrey, in the matter of the corpse with fried feet, as Walter Pritchard put it.

It was Pritchard who recognised the body. So Harry Voyses had bought it after all, he never had much luck. A free-lance operator in a field where only the organisations with real resources could hope to survive. There was a file on him, not much, because Harry had never amounted to much, although he was a smart boy with a safe.

'The last we heard of him,' said Pritchard, 'he was fiddling about on the Middle East stuff. He knew his way round the Israeli v Arab business, and we know that he did some jobs here for the Israelis – nothing big, not that we ever heard about. We had him in on sus once or twice, but there wasn't anything we could pin on him. I rather liked the little feller, he had his code. He wasn't an Israeli, just an active supporter.'

'Not any more,' said Inspector Morton.

'I seem to remember that he married a refugee, from Poland I think,' said Pritchard. 'We'll have an address on the file.'

'So we start to dig,' said Morton, and they drove back up to London.

The Israeli Embassy would of course deny all knowledge of Harry Voyses or what he had been about when he met his death. He would have had no kind of status, officially. Morton would talk in the morning to Leo Grussmann, he decided, once he got the all clear from higher up. If anybody at the Embassy knew about Voyses it would be Grussmann, and since most of the public opinion in the country supported the Israelis, Grussman was likely to be co-operative, within reason.

On the other side of the fence, there were the active Arab nationalists in London, plenty of them, and not short of money either. It was no soft job, trying to keep an eye on them. Controlling the Sunday afternoon demonstrations whenever the Israelis pulled off anything extra saucy, that was the easy part. The real headache was trying to keep tabs on the under-cover groups, guessing what they might be up to.

Violence was in the air. London didn't want to see what other European cities had seen recently – aircraft hi-jacked and blown up, bombs tossed about in public buildings, slaughtering innocent by-standers, all to the greater glory of the United Arab Republic.

It was late the next morning before the niceties of protocol allowed Inspector Morton to be talking with Leo Grussmann, on the neutral territory of a café over cups of coffee that neither of them tasted. Grussmann, bland and polite, was volunteering nothing, and showed only minimal interest in the fate of one Harry Voyses. All of which was to be expected.

They tossed the subject back and forth in a guarded fashion, while their coffees grew cold and muddy.

'I'm going to see the widow,' said Morton. 'Are you coming?'

Grussmann reflected. 'Would that serve any useful purpose, Inspector?'

'Come off it,' said Morton. 'He's dead, Leo. You have a responsibility, and we both know it.'

'What a devious man you are,' said Grussmann.

'I'm just a copper,' said Morton, 'doing my job. And I'm going to do my damnedest to find out who tortured Harry Voyses before he died. If that doesn't appeal to you, if that is no concern of yours, you're not the man I thought you were. She's at home and she's waiting. I haven't told her.'

Morton got up and walked out of the café. He knew he hadn't handled that very well, because Grussmann would need time to get in touch with his bosses and get new briefing.

The interview with Ilse Voyses was one he could well have done without. She made no scene, she didn't cry. But she insisted on seeing the body, and he couldn't persuade her otherwise. He thought he had never seen a woman who looked so absolutely alone in the world.

He could have passed the trip on, but he

drove her himself, and she said nothing to him on the way down. He thought sulphuric thoughts about Leo Grussmann, for what good that did him. Diplomats were a different breed.

Entering the mortuary she said, 'Leave me alone with him, please.'

When she came out her eyes were stony, and all the way back she sat with her hands clasped in her lap, and he knew she saw nothing. She said nothing. And he had the wisdom not to offer any kind of comment, it would have been an intrusion. He felt jaded and arid, after being on all the night before and having missed his lunch by driving her down to see her Harry. There was his interim report to make out for the Superintendent, and even a young and energetic Inspector needs sleep some time.

When they arrived at her place she said, in a flat and lifeless voice, 'Thank you, Inspector. He was always good to me, you know.'

Then she got out of the car and he watched her walk straight-backed and stiff up the steps, and he knew she didn't want him with her, not yet. The door closed. Alone in there with her grief. A hell of a business for women, it always was. Men died and women grieved.

'He was always good to me' – epitaph for a failure. Harry Voyses hadn't made much of a mark in the world. But one woman had loved him. So that couldn't be a failure.

If Inspector Morton had remained there for an hour or so he would have seen the arrival of Leo Grussmann. She let him in, without any greeting. She had gone beyond mere courtesies.

'I'm sorry,' he said. 'I'm more sorry than I can say.'

'I will make coffee,' she said, and walked into the kitchen. He followed and stood in the doorway, watching, while she busied herself. The kitchen was shabby, but spotless, like the rest of the flat. There was nobody to clean it for now, only herself. So far she hadn't glanced at him. He might have been the man come to read the gas meter.

She carried the cups of coffee in on a tray, and put the tray on the table.

'Will you please sit,' she said, 'and help yourself to sugar.'

She sat at her ease, facing him, her hands clasped on the edge of the table.

'Believe me,' he said, 'I know how you must be feeling, Mrs Voyses–'

'You cannot,' she said. 'He was my husband, so how can you know what it is like with me?'

'If there is anything I can do,' he began.

'You cannot bring him back to me,' she said.

'Anything I say will seem like an impertinence,' he said softly, 'but I must tell you how deeply sorry I am personally... I had a great regard for him–'

'–That was not the way you were speaking when you were here last,' she said. 'In your mind you were thinking my husband was cheating you.'

'No,' said Grussmann. Then: 'You must understand that I was acting on the orders of my superiors. I always had confidence in your husband, Mrs Voyses, always.'

'Are you being honest with me now?' she said. 'He was doing your business when he died, you sent him to do something you could not do yourself – that should make you feel guilty ... does it?'

'Yes, and that is partly why I am here.'

'Good,' she said with sharp emphasis. 'What was he doing for you? It must have been important because it cost him his life, and do not tell me it is too delicate a matter to talk about, Mr Leo Grussmann, not any more.'

'He was to get us some information, of a political nature. It was not meant to be dangerous … not unduly dangerous, that is. Your husband was experienced–'

'–Now he is dead. You know what they did to him?'

Grussmann nodded.

'You must know who they were,' she said, 'so what are you going to do?'

'The police have it now, we must leave it to them.'

'You know more than they do,' she said. 'You say it was a political matter.'

'Yes.'

'So you will know who these people are.'

'I have no proof,' he said. 'Not yet.'

She smiled bleakly. 'How many dead bodies do you need?'

'Mrs Voyses,' he said earnestly, 'we will co-operate fully with the police, I promise you that–'

'–Begin with me,' she said. 'Where did he go?'

'I do beg you,' he said, 'leave this to the police.'

'You say you had already given him some money, so you know where he was going – you are not the kind of man to give money away blindly.' Her eyes were as stony as her voice. 'What political information was it that cost my husband his life while you are sitting here alive and well? You are an Israeli, my husband was not ... you are a young man, you have a position and authority – perhaps you have a wife, a family.'

'I have both,' he said soberly.

'I hope you will continue to live to enjoy and protect them, Mr Grussmann.'

He spread his hands. 'As you must know,' he said, 'there are Arab groups here in London, Arab supporters and sympathisers, even Members of Parliament, some prominent people in public life ... the ultimate aim is the elimination of Israel, Nasser has made that clear often enough. We are fighting for survival, as we have always fought, and we need all the information we can gather about our enemies' intentions. Your husband was helping us, he was confident he knew where he could get information that would interest us.'

'So?'

'We have our own under-cover agents, of course, but this was to be something different ... our men are dedicated professionals, but we cannot pretend to know everything that may be going on. I have had dealings with your husband before, and he had never disappointed me. There have been indications that the Arabs might try something out of the ordinary this summer, here in England; there have been a number of new arrivals, allegedly students, but we all know what that covers…'

'You tell me nothing that I cannot read for myself in the newspapers,' she said. 'I am no stranger to persecution myself – I have been a Displaced Person in my time … and now I find myself a widow.'

'We are naturally anxious to help you in any way that we can,' he said. 'Your husband was not one of our regular people, but we do feel a responsibility–'

'You are offering me money?' she interrupted softly.

And Leo Grussmann felt more than uncomfortable under the fixity of her gaze. 'We would like to make some suitable arrangements for you.'

'I can work,' she said harshly. 'So you are telling me nothing? Where my husband went and who was there?'

'I have no details I can give you, Mrs Voyses. Your husband worked alone always. I'm sorry, but there is nothing you can do at this stage.'

She stood up abruptly and walked to the

door. He picked up his hat.

'Your husband mentioned some English-men who are believed to be working for the Arabs, he knew them and he had been watching them... I believe they may have had the information he spoke about.'

'Their names?' she said, holding the door open for him.

'He kept that to himself, I don't believe he ever mentioned their names.'

'Come and see me again,' she said, 'when your memory is better.' Then she showed him out.

SEVEN

The next morning Sam Harris looked up Lockerton in the R.A.C. handbook. It was a small village in Wiltshire near Marlborough, and there was no mention of any military camp, but there was only one Lockerton so this must be it.

The sun was shining, he was a man of substance for a change, and all the day was his to pass as he pleased. Nobody could make him do anything if he didn't fancy it. Independence, that was the thing. There was nothing to take the place of a nice wedge of money.

He could pay off the long-standing instalments on the car, but that was throwing money away because the finance blokes had no idea where he was. Not for one moment did he seriously think of settling some of the back maintenance for that ex-wife of his, let her graft for it like anybody else, the little cow.

He drove up to the West End and selected a mohair job that convinced him again that he had the makings of a dishy hunk of manhood; Italian-type dark glasses added distinction, he thought... Continental film producer stuff. Arty, sexy as all get-out.

Near Porchester Walk he left the car and got a taxi. Down the cobbles and past the pub where he had diddled Ric Bonner, under the arch, he had the driver crawling while he took a good look around; there were the usual parked cars and he thought he knew each of them; if there was anybody watching his flat they weren't visible.

At the end where the Walk looped back on itself there was a blue Volkswagen, the young man sitting at the wheel looked tired and bored, and he wasn't Ric Bonner. He glanced across incuriously as the taxi went past. Another bloody Wog, Sam decided. The place is getting lousy with them. What was he waiting there for? There was a bird operating a call-girl business further down, but she didn't work in the morning; in any case, she wouldn't leave a client waiting outside, he might change his mind and nip off.

So maybe 14b was under observation after all.

Sam gave his driver some instructions so that they drove around and about for a while, then back to Porchester Walk, and the blue Volkswagen was still there, the young man with his dark sulky face was looking really cheesed off by now – little black moustache and dark eyes.

Up yours. Sam had himself driven back to his car, and his driver was sure he was a nut case, especially after Sam dropped him a oncer and wouldn't have any change.

Sam didn't hurry on the way down to Wiltshire, and it was late afternoon when he drove slowly past the main entrance to the camp. The sight of the main guardroom and the tough bastard standing there with his white gaiters and stripes brought back no happy memories. In Sam's view, Military Police were as low as they come, and thick with it. Sling you inside as soon as look at you, and then work up a list of charges as long as your arm.

The Officers' Mess building was easily spotted, with its separate entrance and the crest on the gates: lawns and flowers and the tennis courts, all segregated from the nasty low-class soldiers, striped awnings over the windows.

Sam stopped the car and watched a couple playing tennis. The girl had skinny legs and not much in front; not worth watching.

This looked like the easy way into the camp; there was no guard on the gate here, and while Sam watched, cars with civilian drivers were moving in and out, some parked in front of the building, but some went round the back and appeared lower down on the way into the camp; so there was a road in at the rear; he wouldn't be noticed, and if he was he had a story ready and the right clobber.

He drove sedately round the Mess building, there was a line of garages at the back and the road forked, one going up the rise to the married quarters, the other into the camp; there were plenty of people moving around, including women pushing prams, young men in civvies carrying their weekend cases towards the guardroom, one or two even in uniform – and the best of luck to them as well.

He drove past the deserted parade ground with its flagpole and saluting base; a ragged stooping line of men in denims picked at the tarmac under the supervision of a Corporal, removing moss and weeds that might offend the C.O.'s eye in the morning. Sam could recall one or two similar chores and the grunted language it caused. Frigging fatigues.

The Armoury was a squat building with barred windows, standing at the far end of the area; there was an enclosed yard at the back, but the double doors were open and he saw soldiers shifting ammunition cases about; a tannoy was squawking but nobody seemed to be taking much notice.

The tall barn of a building must be the gymnasium, the only other building nearby. It stood on higher ground and there was a grassy slope, all cut nice and short, like the rest of the camp surrounds – that meant plenty of bull for the boys on domestic nights, like the whitewash on the kerbs and steps. There was a dolly in WRAC uniform, skirt and shirt, sitting on the grass slope, and a soldier lounged at a strategic position below her so that he could observe what might be available later after he had chatted her up.

There was a lone figure on the sports field, in issue shorts and vest, plodding around the track.

Sam drove around and about; he reckoned he'd spent over forty minutes inside the camp, he had seen all he wanted, nobody had said a word to him. He dawdled back past the Armoury and got out of the car; that must be the NAAFI grocery shop along there, there were women and kids about, and a van unloading stuff. He strolled in, James Bond in a mohair suit, and bought cigarettes. He was tempted to walk into the Sergeants' Mess, just for the hell of it.

He went back to the car; the WRAC dolly had gone, and so had the ambitious soldier. On the edge of the parade ground some sweating lads were going through fire drill, running out the hoses like crazy, and getting themselves cussed by the Corporal who didn't do much moving himself. Happy days in the peace-time Army.

Sam left the way he had entered; there was music from the open windows of the Officers' Mess; agile young blokes in shorts were banging about on the tennis courts. He stopped the car, got out, and with a thoughtful air checked the roses in the flower bed. All you needed was a bit of nerve and you could help yourself to anything you fancied at Lockerton camp, in and out with no bother.

The village was half a mile down the road, not much of a place, a few shops, two pubs – one much smarter than the other, called itself 'The Lockerton Hotel'. This was the one the officers of the camp were likely to use. It had a dining-room and a menu on show outside the door, set in a brass frame. RAC and AA appointed.

It was just after opening time, there were cars parked in the rear, including a white Mini. Sam parked and strolled into the lounge, and then did a smart about-turn back into the hall. Stone the crows. Ric Bonner was in there, sitting by the window talking to another bloke. He hadn't looked up; they had drinks on the table.

Sam slipped into the saloon bar and bought a whisky. There was a door out to the parking place and the gents, and he could watch the lounge. He might have walked slap into a mess... Ric Bonner wasn't down there for the air or the scenery. Sam wondered who the other bloke was, he wasn't the old goat with the lame leg and the stick. He wondered still more if Sophie was in the party ... the dark glasses and the mohair clobber wouldn't fool Sophie. It wasn't a nice thought. Maybe he should push off while he could. He thought of the fifteen hundred quid.

Ric Bonner looked at his watch and stood up. 'He's not coming,' he said softly. 'So we'll go to him, come on.'

'He won't like that,' said Henry Timmins.

'Then he'll have to do the other thing.'

They left the lounge and Sam saw them cross the hall. He took a cautious look, they were both getting into the Mini and that Bonner looked as sour as hell. Sam sidled towards the door.

Bonner drove out into the village street, over the bridge over the disused railway line where the village straggled to nothing but a few houses. A few hundred yards along there was a bungalow set back from the road, a little box of a place, cheap and unlovely, and needing repair.

There was a rickety gate and a narrow path up to the door; the small patch of front garden was over-grown, and only the curtains at the windows hinted that the place was occupied. Somewhere in the rear chickens made disgruntled noises.

'You'd think he'd clean the place up a bit,' said Timmins. Bonner shrugged and led the way up the path.

The front door bell should have made a *ding-dong* chime, but all they heard was a muted *ding*. Typical, nothing in the place would work properly.

Fred Halley opened the door, with his habitual worried expression. He was forty-two but looked much older – a man who would always find circumstances too much for him, a born loser; even his straggling moustache lacked conviction. Yet there must have been a spark of spirit about him sometimes, because he had married two wives and had fathered six children, and providing for this brood kept him poor and depressed. He was a clerk in the Orderly Room at the camp, a low grade civilian clerk, the kind who is always passed over for promotion.

He wore a loose cardigan, his office trousers, and tartan slippers, with holes cut to accommodate his bunions.

'I was just about to come down,' he said.

'We saved you the trouble,' said Bonner. 'May we come in?'

Halley showed them into the front room, shuffling along like an arthritic old gent. There was a strong smell of frying fish from the back, and the sound of kids whimpering.

The room was small and square and stuffed with bits of furniture that were meant for a larger room – items salvaged by Halley from his first marital home when his first wife left him.

Watery-eyed, self-effacing, full of apologies, Fred Halley looked anything but a stallion, but there was no doubting his fertility or his abnormal success with women, some women.

He was about to shut the door when a very pregnant youngish woman looked into the room, nodded at the visitors, and said to her husband, 'Tea's ready, don't be long.'

'No dear,' said Halley and shut the door, and it was clear he would have preferred to follow his wife out.

'Well,' said Bonner, 'what's happening? Anything unusual at your end?'

'Just normal,' said Halley. The three of them, together with the furniture, crowded the little room.

'Good,' said Bonner, 'we'll have to keep it like that. Any special movements I ought to know about? What about that north gate? Are they using it?'

'It's closed,' said Halley. 'They're laying a water main or something like that, and they closed the road. It'll be shut some time. But I checked on Lieutenant Dunne, he'll be away as from Thursday, playing cricket. Warrant Officer Ransome will be taking the Armoury over temporarily.'

'I knew a Sergeant Tommy Ransome,' said Timmins, 'would it be the same one? Fat feller with a red face, likes his wallop?'

Halley nodded, still anxious to please. 'Just posted in from the depot.'

'That'll mess things,' said Timmins to Bonner. 'Tommy Ransome will recognise me soon as he sees me – I don't fancy that one little bit.'

'The Colonel will be on leave next week,' said Halley. 'Major Hetherington will be taking the parade on the Saturday, and he don't bother too much– Ransome won't be on camp much after 1100, he nips off early when it's safe.'

Halley dug in his trouser pocket and brought out a folded sheet of paper and offered it to Bonner. 'I was doing the duty list,' he said, 'so I copied the roster, Captain Baines is on next week-end, he don't let it worry him much, he'll be in the Mess most of the time.'

'No draft due in or out next week-end?' said Bonner.

'No,' said Halley. 'We're well below strength, what with the leave period being on and that...' He paused, and said, 'Mr Bonner, you promised I'd be all right, I don't want no trouble ... you did promise you'd see me right...'

Bonner took out his wallet and very carefully took out four five pound notes, he folded them and placed them on the mantelpiece. 'Don't be on the camp,' he said. 'Go sick. That'll let you out.'

'I been thinking,' said Halley, hesitantly–

'–Don't,' said Bonner. 'You know nothing about it, right?' He smiled pleasantly. 'If anything leaked out and they traced it back to you, now that wouldn't be nice for you, would it? You are a Government employee, in a position of trust … you'd get ten years at least.'

Fred Halley swallowed. Through the thin wall the voice of his ever-loving wife was in anger at one of her complaining brats. As always, Halley felt himself surrounded by impending and inescapable doom. There was never enough money to go round … six kids, pretty soon there'd be seven, two women.

He heard Bonner's soft voice repeating: 'You know nothing…'

'The wife don't like it,' he said. 'She knows something's up … you know what they're like when they're expecting, all nerves like…'

'I wouldn't know about that,' said Bonner placidly.

'It makes things difficult for me,' said Halley.

'Give her the money,' said Bonner, 'not

the bookie, that'll sweeten her ... and don't tell her anything. Now is there anything else I ought to know about?'

'I don't think so.' Halley sounded quite unhappy. 'There isn't going to be any trouble, is there? I don't want to be mixed up in any trouble...'

Bonner patted his shoulder. 'No trouble,' he said. 'Be on the bridge, this side of it, next Wednesday, sharp at seven-thirty, rain or shine. I'll be driving the same car, and don't keep me waiting or there won't be any money, you hear?'

There was a rapping on the wall, and a strident voice called: *Fr-e-e-d!* It's on the table!'

Fred Halley let them out, muttering some kind of an apology. Fried mackerel for tea, that was evident.

'Wednesday,' said Bonner sociably. 'Seven-thirty. Cheer up.'

Fred Halley watched them go down the path and get into the little white car, then turned back into the room. He was too late, the money wasn't there on the mantelpiece any more. She had got her hooks on it sharp enough. You just couldn't win. And fried mackerel always gave him the gripes.

Sam Harris allowed the Mini to get a discreet distance in front before following. Bonner and the other bloke had been grinning like hell about something when they got into the car, and they weren't driving too fast. He hoped they might be driving back to London, because Sam felt more at home there, not so exposed. Furthermore he was hungry.

'We'll just check the place where we swap vehicles,' said Bonner. 'It's the best I could find.'

They turned up a lane that ran in through a coppice at the foot of a gentle hill where they could see the fallen stumps of trees; up along a bumpy track they came to a clearing with a large open-sided shed.

'They haven't worked here for months,' said Bonner.

Timmins got out and walked about the clearing. 'Fifteen minutes easy drive from the camp,' he said. 'Ideal, I reckon.'

'Why else do you think I picked it?' said Bonner. 'It's tailor-made for us.'

It was very quiet, very secluded, there were no farm buildings near, wood pigeons cooed in the trees, and on the long side of the hill the evening sun was soft and golden.

'That Fred Halley, he makes me edgy,' said Timmins. 'He's too scared.'

'I'll scare him some more next Wednesday,' said Bonner. 'We've got all we need from him ... he's a loser all the way, don't give him another thought – we couldn't have found a better mug: up to his ears in debt, and no guts – and a snug little job right inside the camp headquarters, he's a natural for us, so we'll have to keep him scared, good for his soul.'

'Maybe,' said Timmins. 'But I wouldn't push him too far, though. I've seen his sort fold up.'

Bonner tapped him on the chest, lightly. 'Worry about your end of it, leave the rest to me, right?'

Sam Harris had stopped on the road, just beyond the lane; native caution had warned him not to follow them up there because it wouldn't lead anywhere important, and if he met them head-on he would be in the clag. So he exercised his talent for waiting. A little traffic went past, not much but enough to make him feel less prominent, parked there on the roadside.

He heard the Mini coming down, it went past him and he straightened up and followed. There was nothing spectacular about their speed, and Sam had no trouble keeping his place. Along the wide main street in Marlborough, up the hill and through the Forest, and a faster run into Hungerford.

They pulled in at 'The Bear', took on petrol, parked the Mini and went into the hotel. Sam filled his tank, speculated about the chance of getting something himself, and decided against. They weren't inside very long, just a quick snort.

Now they were humming along rather more smartly, but they didn't shake Sam. The other side of Reading he nearly lost them because another white Mini intruded, and with the thickening traffic he had to make sure he was after the right one, and everybody was in the usual hurry.

By Heathrow the Mini cut across and went down on the Staines road. On the outskirts of the town the Mini stopped, and Sam watched while Bonner's passenger got out, had a quick final word with Bonner, then walked on into the town. The Mini pulled away, and so did Sam.

Along by Kempton Park, then into the back streets of Feltham. Tricky driving because Bonner knew where he was going and Sam didn't. The streets were narrow and littered with parked vehicles; there were kids playing in the roadway; pubs on the corners; fish and chip shops; definitely low class.

Eventually Bonner parked alongside a high wall and let himself in a door, using a key and locking it after him. Doodling past, Sam stopped. The place looked derelict, but he knew it wasn't or Bonner wouldn't be there.

Bonner was half an hour inside there. Sam had parked by an abandoned car with no wheels and no doors. It was nearly ten and the pub up the road sounded as though it was doing good and merry business. Sam could have done with a pint of old and mild and a pie. He stayed put.

He followed the Mini into Twickenham, where Bonner got out and made a call at a phone box, then on over the river and into Chiswick. When the Mini went along a side road behind some tall houses and then turned in a gate, Sam guessed they had come to the end for the time being. He heard the tall gates slam, the revving of an engine, then silence. So Bonner was probably in for the night.

It was a big place, big enough for a hotel or a hostel, from what he could see. He promised himself another look, then drove off for food – not a pint of wallop and a pie, real nosh, he could afford it, and it had been a long day.

EIGHT

Sam Harris's luck later that night was better than he had hoped for. Feltham seemed a softer touch than the big house in Chiswick, and he was just pulling up by the derelict car when he saw the Army truck coming out. Fenna was doing a quick road test, and the sight of a civilian driver taking an Army truck out of a dump like that convinced Sam that he hadn't made a wrong guess.

He watched the tail lights of the truck disappear down the road, then gave his attention to the wall. By standing on the top of the derelict car he could get both elbows on the top of the wall, and he swung himself up. It did the pricey mohair suit no good. There was a ten foot drop. He managed it neatly enough.

There was plenty of timber lying around, and some packing cases; he piled them against the inside of the wall, for his exit. Always make sure of the way out – Sam had got himself clobbered before in a no-exit situation, and there was no future in it.

He picked his way across the yard to the double-doors of what looked like a warehouse. A small door had been cut in one side, with a Yale lock. Sam fished in his wallet for the thin tapering piece of perspex – there wasn't a copper in the country who could prove it was a house-breaking tool, not *prove* it.

He tickled the lock and opened the door and stepped into the darkness inside, and he could still smell the exhaust fumes of the truck. He found the switch on the wall. This was a very well equipped workshop, this was no junk yard, somebody had been spending money here.

He walked around the Humber staff car; pretty good, the real thing, it would fool anybody … tucked away in a back street outfit in Feltham, and little Sammie knew all about it.

So how could he handle the situation to extract the maximum of profit? There had to be a profit in it somewhere. The key was in the Humber – he could knock it off and see what happened? Let them sweat a little and put on some pressure? Sam savoured the prospect.

Then he heard the sound of a heavy engine outside in the road. He jumped for the light switch as he heard the scrape of the outside doors opening. He ducked behind the Humber, there was nowhere else in the dark. Something clinked under his foot, a handy spanner. He latched onto it – he might need something. He shouldn't have been hanging around in there, he should have scarpered as soon as he saw what they had.

The double doors opened and the headlights lit up the place as the truck came easing in with a lot of *vroom-vroom* that deafened him. It stopped right behind the Humber, and Sam edged away to the other side, crouching double … the doors were still open and he thought he just might make a run for it.

But the blasted driver got out and went over and put the main lights on. He came back to the truck and switched off the engine and the headlights, and Sam couldn't guess which side he was going to move then.

He guessed wrong, so that he met the driver, in between the Humber and the truck, and the surprise was mutual.

'Hey you!' said Fenna. 'What are you…?'

Sam jumped into action and tried to dart to one side, but there was oil on the floor and he slipped. Fenna grabbed him, they rolled about on the floor, and Sam wasn't winning. He still had the spanner, but Fenna was younger and much more active, and he had seen the spanner.

They banged up against the rear wheel of the truck, with Fenna on the inside berth for the moment, so Sam was able to slam his head hard against the rim, and he heard Fenna grunt and felt his grip slacken, just a little. He swung the spanner at Fenna's head, but got his shoulder instead, and Fenna squealed like a puppy that had been trodden on.

Sam scrambled away, dropped the spanner, and ran like hell to the open door, and he didn't look back. He got up over the wall and dropped down and ran to his car, and he didn't relax until he had done a couple of quick miles. The mohair was ruined, and he had a couple of bruises ... without that spanner he wouldn't have made it. He was glad it hadn't been that Ric Bonner he had been tangling with.

That would have to do for one night. He was still the boy on top of the heap. That would throw a scare into them, wondering just how he happened to be inside there ... who he was, and how much he knew. Sam Harris, man of mystery.

The night porter was on at the hotel and was most concerned at Sam's appearance, so Sam told him he'd had a little trouble with the car. The bar was shut, but the porter was happy to get Sam a very large whisky, because the word had got about that this funny little character with the ginger hair was a free spender.

Sam dropped the porter a couple of quid to take the suit and get it to the cleaners the first thing in the morning, then, with most of the large whisky sloshing about inside him, he soaked in a hot bath and wondered if the job might not be too big to swing alone, and he couldn't think of anybody who wouldn't diddle him in the end, which was a fitting comment on his friends and associates.

Ted Fenna sat alone for some minutes after Sam Harris had departed. He hadn't been badly hurt, his shoulder ached, and there was a bump on the back of his head. He had never been the athletic type, and he had never seen any point in football or boxing or any other contact sport, and he knew that if his reflexes had been sharper, he wouldn't have been so roughly handled.

He wasn't supposed to contact Bonner except in an emergency; he had a phone number, and if this wasn't an emergency Fenna was very much mistaken. He rang the number, Hugo Essard answered and took the message, and inside forty minutes Bonner was with Fenna in the warehouse.

Nothing had been taken, Fenna was sure of that. 'I wasn't out of here more than ten minutes,' he said. 'There wasn't time for him to nick anything, and we got stuff worth pinching, those two new heavy duty tyres for a start, and my tools.'

'And he was alone?' said Bonner.

'That's right, took me by surprise and thumped me with that spanner, a nasty little bastard with crinkly ginger hair, real mean... I dunno how the hell he got in because I left it all locked up, always do.'

'Probably just some casual prowler,' said Bonner. He knew very well it wasn't, the description fitted the man who had been engaging their attention, but it wouldn't do to tell Fenna that – if Fenna knew there had been a leak he might get cold feet, and that wouldn't do now, they needed him.

'It must have been some fly boy who noticed you working here late at night, and got inquisitive ... you scared him off before he could take anything, nothing to worry about.'

Fenna indicated the two vehicles. 'What about them? He saw them, Army jobs, he'll wonder what they were doing in here.'

'We're on an Army sub-contracting job,' said Bonner. 'He won't think anything about it ... anyway, he's just a burglar who picked the wrong spot to break in, he got nothing, so he won't be back.'

'I hope not,' said Fenna. 'I won't fancy working here at night if there's going to be any more of this. He was proper vicious, he was.'

'We'll get a better lock for that door,' said Bonner. 'Make sure both vehicles are immobilised before you leave at night.'

'Always do,' said Fenna.

'You're doing a good job,' said Bonner. 'I'll let the chief know about it.'

Fenna shrugged. He had heard about this 'chief', the man who was putting up the cash, but he knew nothing about him, not even his name. That was the way they wanted it, and it didn't bother Ted Fenna. The money was always on time and no questions.

Doctor Aristide Apian sat at his desk, in cream silk pyjamas and a black dressing-gown; his black hair was smooth, the dark stubble of his beard had begun to show, but his eyes were alert and very watchful; it was a few minutes short of two in the morning.

'It is as I said,' he repeated. 'The man is a professional and he knows exactly what he is doing, because he has the information supplied by Voyses, information taken from your safe, Bonner, so we cannot feel happy while he is at liberty, we have to find him.'

'How?' said Bonner. 'You've had men watching his place in Porchester Walk all day and he hasn't been near it. He's new, and we haven't a line on him. If he was associated with Voyses we never heard about it.'

'There are many things you have never heard about,' said Apian, quite politely, 'and information is of the first importance to us.'

'I do my job,' said Bonner. 'I'm not a machine. I've shifted everybody who matters, including Tessie Raikes.'

Apian lifted one shoulder fastidiously. 'A pity we have to use such coarse material.'

'Sophie wouldn't do it,' said Bonner. 'She's too scared. Tessie's a natural for the job.'

Their eyes met over the width of the desk. Sophie had other qualities of which both were aware, and Apian was the first to lower his glance.

'I think Voyses has been found,' he said softly.

'Hell,' said Bonner. 'What makes you think that?'

'His wife had a visit yesterday afternoon, and we are sure it was a police officer, they went off in a car and they were away some hours. Later she had another visitor. Leo Grussmann, from their Embassy... I don't like any of that, do you?'

Bonner didn't answer, he didn't need to.

'The body could not have been very well hidden,' said Apian. 'It didn't take them long to find it.'

'We did the best we could, there wasn't much time. What do we do now?'

'We will all remain quiet for a while,' said Apian.

'Are you going to scrub it?' said Bonner.

'I think not.'

'If this Harris character was working with Voyses,' said Bonner, 'something will start happening when he knows Voyses is dead, he might even tell the police, we know nothing about him, he didn't impress me much that night.'

'Which shows how good he is.' Apian smiled. 'The location of Fenna's workshop was not with the papers Voyses took, so how did this Harris know where to go? Give that a little thought, Bonner – believe me, this man is clever, I am more concerned about him than I am about Grussmann, and you had him in your hands that night and you let him go.'

Ric Bonner lit a cigarette and almost stifled a yawn. He was fed up to the teeth hearing about Harris and what he should have done with him.

'We will do nothing for a few days,' said Apian. 'I have told Essard to move out, and you will do the same. You will only come here after dark and after clearing with me by telephone, otherwise nothing will be changed. You might give some attention to Fenna at night–'

'–We ought to move the workshop,' said Bonner.

'All right,' said Apian. 'Find another place, do it in the morning, keep Fenna working – and happy. He is still important to us. Watch the newspapers for anything about Voyses … and think about this man Harris – my instructions are that we must find him quickly, I am using every man I have, and that must include you.' Apian smiled. 'You may not be one of us, Bonner, but you have been taking our money – and money is important to you, the kind of money I have been giving you. There is more to come, much more, if I am satisfied.'

'You'll be satisfied,' said Bonner. 'Anything else?'

'Nothing at the moment, but keep in touch with me.'

Little Napoleon in pansy silk pyjamas, Bonner thought as he rose to leave. He wanted to ask where Sophie was, but he didn't like what the answer might be. Tessie would put him up for what was left of the night, and be glad to do it. Just one more week to wait, then deliver the goods and collect the cash, the last large slice that would make it all worth while. Then he would kiss Aristide Apian goodbye and read all about it in the papers – another outrage by Arab terrorists, if they didn't mess it up.

He drove the white Mini round to Leinster Gardens, and woke Tessie. She asked no silly questions, she accepted his presence in her bed in the double room she had so thoughtfully taken as a bonus, and an encouraging proof that she could still get a man, which was very good for her morale.

Later, while he slept so soundly beside her, Tessie began to think about the proposed vacation in Majorca. Maybe Ric would be with her. Now that would be something like a holiday, the two of them together in that sunshine, on a beach, living it up, not a care in the world.

She slipped an arm under his shoulders. Come to mamma. Ric grunted and turned away, without waking. What a man. He had said something about moving in with her for a while, so she wouldn't have to rush things … just let him see he wouldn't get better loving anywhere else. He must have split with that Sophie – whose bed was he in anyway?

Tessie slept contentedly. All would be well.

Two phone calls that night had reached Hugo Essard alone in the flat. The first had been from the very agitated Ted Fenna with the disturbing news about an intruder in the workshop, to be passed on to Ric Bonner at Chiswick, which Essard had done. Then later Apian had called, very busy and brusque – Essard was to get out of the flat forthwith and to remain immobile and quiet for a few days – an instruction which Essard had been expecting ever since there had been that nonsense on the stairs with Harris. It was an obvious precaution.

He would put up at his club, temporarily. The flat had been rented furnished, and Essard spent ten minutes methodically making sure there were no papers left behind. Harry Voyses had taken the only important stuff from the safe in the living-room – the safe installed at Apian's express order and paid for by him, and what a waste of money that had been.

Essard made a selection from his wardrobe and packed two cases, there was no sense in abandoning good clothes. He was taking a last look round when the front door bell rang.

He opened the door to find two smiling young men in quite respectable suits. They saw the cases in the hall just inside the door. The taller one nodded.

'Good,' he said. 'Then you are ready to come with us.'

'Pretty well,' said Essard. 'The Doctor didn't say he was sending anybody for me, I was going to get a taxi.'

'There will be no need, we have a car waiting.'

'Splendid,' said Essard. 'Very thoughtful of the Doctor. I've cleared the place out ... it's been a bit of a rush, but I'm ready–'

'Is Mr Bonner not here as well?' The taller one was doing all the talking; his companion, stocky and dark, had picked up both cases.

'He's with Fenna,' said Essard. 'Didn't

Apian tell you?'

The taller one shrugged, smiling. 'We just do the errands.' He walked past Essard into the flat, did a quick inspection, turning out the lights as he progressed.

'Satisfactory,' he said. 'Shall we go?'

Essard took up his hat and stick. 'You two must be new arrivals, I've never seen you before.'

'We come and we go, it is part of our job ... you are sure Bonner will not be coming back here?'

'No,' said Essard. 'We're all moving tonight, one of those panics, you know.'

'Which is why we should hurry.'

They went out, the two young men took a case each. 'Most kind of you,' said Essard. 'I'm going to my club, The Nondescripts – do you know it?'

'We will find it.'

They filed into the small lift, Essard in the middle. They said nothing going down. A pair of very pleasant and obliging errand boys.

The car was a Ford Escort utility, blue. The stocky one drove, the other sat beside Essard in the back, and they took off fast through fairly empty streets. Essard tried to make some small talk, but got little response;

either they didn't know much or they were being extra cautious because they knew he wasn't really one of them.

After a while he noticed the route they were taking.

'You'll never get to The Nondescript this way,' he said. 'You ought to be heading across to the Old Brompton Road–'

'–We have a call to make first ... you don't mind?'

Something in the way the question sounded made Essard glance over at his companion – he was smiling, a handsome young man with dark eyes and good teeth, fit and strong evidently, a much better specimen than most of Apian's crew.

They had been travelling over half an hour before Essard became just a little concerned; they were going miles out of the way ... but no doubt this was something Aristide Apian had arranged – he didn't believe in giving out too much information. It was amusing, really.

They stopped outside a very ordinary house somewhere in the suburbs, a detached villa in a quiet little road, with a short drive up to the garage ... white gates, crazy paving, little flower beds, all very neat.

They ran the car into the garage. This must

be another new place Apian had taken on, he was spreading himself, Essard reflected as he got out of the car and followed the tall young man through a side door. He was hoping they weren't going to be too long.

They went into a small room, brightly lit with strip lighting and heavily curtained; it was an office of sorts, with a desk and a phone and some wooden chairs; one wall was covered with maps. It all had a make-shift air, like requisitioned premises in an occupied zone. There was no carpet, just bare boards.

A youngish man in a dazzling white shirt and without a tie sat at the desk and looked up as they came in. Essard held out his hand.

'Good evening,' he said. 'We haven't met, I'm Hugo Essard.'

His hand was ignored.

'I am Leo Grussmann,' said the man at the desk. 'Where is Bonner?'

The man beside Essard swung a chair over and planted him in it. 'This was the only one we found there, Leo. He was leaving, so we brought him. I haven't talked to him … he thinks Apian sent us.'

Grussman came round the desk, smiling, to stand over Essard. 'Very amusing,' he said.

'What on earth is this?' demanded Essard.

'This is the other side of the fence, Mister Hugo Essard, and you have strayed over it.'

Essard glanced around the room. When he tried to rise he was planted back into the chair, not too gently.

'Is this a joke?' he said. 'Will somebody please explain – who are you?'

'I have told you,' said Grussmann. 'Now you find yourself in the other camp, and we need some information from you.'

'You are mistaken,' said Essard quickly. 'I have no information, I know nothing. Bonner is a young man of my acquaintance, but I am not concerned in his affairs... I have no idea what you are talking about.'

Grussmann nodded. 'Very pat. Do you know what was done to Harry Voyses?'

Essard kept his eyes on the knob of his walking stick standing up between his knees.

'Tell me about this Doctor Apian,' said Grussmann. 'What is he planning and where does Bonner come into it?'

'I know nothing,' said Essard.

'Something is being planned, we know that much,' said Grussmann. 'That was why Voyses was killed.'

'I never met the man,' said Essard

promptly. 'I know nothing about him, nothing.'

'But you know how he died,' said Grussmann. 'And you know why.'

Essard shook his head, what was the use of talking.

'There is to be more sabotage,' said Grussmann. 'You will tell me where and what form it will take.'

'I can tell you nothing,' said Essard.

'Then we must entertain you to the best of our ability,' said Grussmann. 'I hope your feet are in good condition.'

'You wouldn't do that,' said Essard, gripping the knob of his stick convulsively.

'Where is Bonner now?'

'Probably with Apian ... I don't know – I haven't seen him for two or three days...'

'He is just an acquaintance of yours,' said Grussmann. 'So is this Doctor Apian – you have some strange friends... I am going to enjoy talking to you, I think. There was a case similar to yours, Essard, an Englishman who got ten years for the kind of business you are in, last year. An English judge in an English court of justice gave him ten years for attempted sabotage of an aircraft, and you will remember what the judge called him – a mercenary saboteur, the lowest of the low, willing to kill indiscriminately for money, without even the excuse of a national cause ... that is your rating, Hugo Essard.'

Essard shook his head, sweating, not daring to look up at the man who stood over him, and he was thinking of what they had said about Voyses, what Bonner had said ... they couldn't do that to him, it was unthinkable.

Grussmann yawned and began to roll down his shirt sleeves like a man who has come to the end of a hard day's work.

'I think that will do for now,' he said.

Hugo Essard didn't like the sound of that. He had walked right into this, and it wasn't over. If only he had left the flat five minutes earlier. There was an injustice about this somewhere – it shouldn't have depended on an unlucky accident.

Leo Grussmann was looking at him with evident disgust.

'A gentleman lackey,' he said. 'I have a meeting with police officers in the morning, I don't think I will mention that we have you.'

Essard liked that even less. 'You cannot keep me here,' he said. 'It's too ridiculous.'

'It would be ridiculous to let you go,' said Grussmann. 'We must have our pound of flesh.'

Hugo Essard shuddered. Grussmann nodded and walked out. Essard was yanked up out of his chair and taken out into a small hall, and his legs were feeling very uncertain, but the young man with him helped him and urged him up some stairs, carpeted this time.

'I – I have to use the bathroom.' Essard's voice was nothing like as fruity as normal. He was taken into the bathroom at the top of the stairs, and the young man came in with him and waited, not in the least embarrassed. Then they went into a small room at the rear of the house. It had once been a nursery, there were thin bars on the window, and round the wall there was a jolly frieze featuring Goldilocks and Snow White and Little Red Riding Hood.

The only furniture was a bed against one wall. Essard's cases were on the floor, they had been opened and their contents messed about. Before Essard could make much of a protest the young man quickly searched him and took his cigarettes and matches.

'Is that quite necessary?' said Essard.

'You might set fire to the place, and we can't have that, can we? You will also find it pointless to try shouting out of that window, even if you can get it open – the house on one side is empty and the people on the other side are elderly and rather deaf, so be philosophic about it, Hugo Essard, it is the fortunes of war.' The young man went out and locked the door.

Essard sat disconsolately on the edge of the bed, and he felt suddenly cold, and he knew he would never be able to sleep.

He could hear distant traffic noises, but they afforded him little comfort. Aristide Apian had been so sure that their operations were unknown, secure, unsuspected... Aristide Apian should be sitting here – and Ric Bonner.

The door opened and the young man came in. He had a glass of water in one hand and a couple of pale yellow pills in the other. He held out both to Essard.

'You won't sleep otherwise,' he said, 'and if you don't sleep you'll go off your head.'

Essard hesitated. 'How do I know what they are?' he said. 'They might be poison.'

'You'd be no good to us dead, not yet. We have other plans about you.'

Essard took the pills and washed them down with the water. 'I'd like a cigarette,' he said. 'I can't burn the place down with one cigarette.'

'Perhaps tomorrow, if you're really co-operative.'

Essard glared helplessly at the closing door, heard the key turn in the lock. The bed had a mattress, a bolster, and one thin blanket. He took off his shoes and jacket, and already his movements were becoming uncertain, his head woolly. Fifteen minutes later the young man looked in, found him sleeping, and put the light out. Hugo Essard would keep until they needed him again.

NINE

It was a case of homicide with some unusual features, so far not to be disclosed to the press – that was the official view. Harry Voyses dead was arousing much more interest than he had ever aroused when alive.

Inspector Charles Morton had made his report to his Superintendent, and the word had been duly passed on up the line to those who could do something about it: Leo Grussmann was being less than co-operative in the matter.

'Too bloody cagey by half,' had been Morton's comment to his superior. 'It's not like him to hold back on us, but he knows more than he lets on ... Harry Voyses was his boy...'

Eventually the Special Branch Commander himself was listening to Morton. Relations with the Embassy had always been good, and the Commander agreed with young Morton that the death of Harry Voyses was no run-of-the-mill killing. So if Leo Grussmann knew anything about it, the

Commander promised to see that representations would be made in the right quarter, discreet but sharpish.

The result was that Leo Grussmann on the Saturday afternoon was sitting in Morton's office, the picture of diplomatic good-will, in a suit of clothes that no police Inspector could ever hope to afford honestly on his pay.

Grussmann said he had been to see Mrs Voyses, and since then certain information had come his way – he had a name and an address that might connect with Voyses. Voyses had in fact mentioned an Englishman named Richard Bonner, with an address in the West End, which Grussmann gave to Morton.

'You've already been there,' said Morton. 'Don't tell me you waited until now.'

'Some of our people did look in there last night,' said Grussmann. 'There was nobody there.'

'There wouldn't be,' said Morton. 'Any details about this Richard Bonner?'

'Nothing much,' said Grussmann. 'Voyses wasn't very talkative, but I gathered that Bonner was another outsider who had come into the business recently.'

'You haven't told me yet what Voyses was

supposed to be doing for you,' said Morton.

Grussmann looked at Morton with dark unfathomable eyes, just a little sad and contemplative. 'I cannot remember saying that he worked for us.'

'You didn't need to,' said Morton. 'I think we must get one thing clear between us – this is a homicide.'

'Evidently,' said Grussmann.

'We are going to dig away at it, and to hell with protocol. Agreed?'

Grussmann smiled gently. 'Quite. We are on the same side in this.'

'I wonder about that,' said Morton.

'An unfriendly thought, my dear Inspector, we have always co-operated in the past, haven't we?'

'You have,' said Morton. 'Which makes me all the more certain that you're back-pedalling this time … so just don't get in my way.'

Presently Leo Grussmann left without adding anything more that might be of interest, Morton and Sergeant Pritchard drove to Richard Bonner's address.

It was a beautiful afternoon. 'My rest day,' said Pritchard, 'another myth – I was supposed to take the kids swimming.'

'Not a hope,' said Morton.

'That's a smooth boy, that Grussmann,' said Pritchard. 'I don't think I ever heard a nicer liar.'

'That's diplomacy at work,' said Morton.

There was of course no answer when they rang the bell at Bonner's flat. Pritchard went in search of the caretaker and found his little domicile on the ground floor beyond the arcade where the shops were doing nice business on a Saturday afternoon. The caretaker was out, he would be, and his wife had nothing to say – she had never even seen Bonner, she said. The flat had been sub-let furnished, she knew that much ... most of the tenants were short-term visitors to London who didn't fancy living in a hotel.

Pritchard rejoined his chief and took out his keys. Morton gave him a nod. They went in. The flat had three bedrooms and a large living-room, kitchen and bathroom; good quality furniture, fitted carpets; one of the bedrooms had been used by a woman, a young woman, to judge from the clothes in the wardrobe. The other two were men's rooms. There was food in the fridge, not much, which suggested that the occupants mostly ate out.

All the signs were that there had been a

hurried departure; there were no letters about, no papers; in a drawer of the bedside table in one of the rooms there was paperback with the name 'Ric Bonner' scrawled in the front.

The beds had been made but the flat hadn't been dusted for some little time; there were vases of dead flowers, ashtrays that hadn't been emptied.

'Curtains all drawn,' said Pritchard. 'So they left last night, after dark.'

In the living-room Morton squatted in front of a miniature safe, a small de luxe model that should have been fitted into a wall, the kind of safe the lady of the house has hidden behind a picture in her bedroom to take her jewels. This one sat on a bracket with a bookcase in front of it. It was locked.

'This didn't come with the furniture,' said Morton. 'There'll be nothing in it when we get it opened. Wally, you get on to the agents who let the place and see what they can tell us about the last tenants here.'

'Be a nice surprise for them,' said Pritchard. 'They don't know they've got a vacancy, and I'll lay a week's pay there's no safe in the inventory.'

The phone rang. Morton picked it up, and a woman's voice asked if she could speak to

Mr Hugo Essard.

'I'm afraid he's not in at the moment,' said Morton. 'Can I take a message?'

'Would you tell him I called – this is Myra Foster, I'm in the flat on the floor below, he'll remember... I was wondering if he'd care to drop in for a drink one evening, soon – when do you expect him back?'

'Difficult to say,' said Morton. 'But I'll make sure he gets your invitation, Miss Foster.'

'Thank you so much,' she said. 'It's Mrs actually.'

'My apologies, Mrs Foster.'

Morton put the phone down. 'So now we have another name,' he said. 'That was the lady from downstairs inviting Hugo Essard for a drink... Hugo Essard – does that ring a bell with you?'

'Not a thing,' said Wally Pritchard. 'He must be another new boy. The flat was probably taken in his name.'

'Bonner and Essard,' said Morton. 'That explains two of the bedrooms, and there's a woman in the case.'

'Always is,' said Pritchard. 'A dolly bird, most likely.'

In the hall as they were leaving it was

Morton who noticed the mark high up on the wall; there was a straight groove cutting into the plaster and a small hole in the facing wall directly in line with the groove. He had to stand on a chair to pick at the hole with the point of his penknife blade. He showed Pritchard the small slug he had dug out of the plaster.

Pritchard measured the height of the hole. 'He wasn't much of a shot if he was trying to hit anybody.'

'Could have been a fight,' said Morton. 'That hole is fairly new, I think.' He put the bullet into an envelope. And before they left the flat they gave it another and more intensive search, without any result – beyond proof in the bathroom cabinet that the unnamed lady who made up the trio was either married or ought to be.

Myra Foster was pleasantly surprised when she opened her door and found two males there, and one of them was not at all bad-looking in a healthy sort of way. And she was distinctly intrigued to hear that they were police officers, one of them an Inspector, the nice young one. They were making enquiries and they thought she might be able to help them, if she would be so good…

'Do please come in,' said Myra, and led them into her sitting-room. She had been rather expecting Sam, but this might be more interesting.

They sat and Myra gave them a nice display of her nice legs in a mini that few women of her age could dare to wear.

'We're interested in the people in the flat above yours, Mrs Foster,' said Morton. 'When you rang just now and asked for Hugo Essard I answered the phone – how well do you know him?'

Myra's eyes widened with delight. 'Don't tell me he's in trouble, and I thought he was such a gentleman, really ... to tell you the truth I didn't know him all that well, but I had met him – what has he done, Inspector?'

'We don't know,' said Morton patiently. 'Could you describe him?'

'Oh, middle-aged,' said Myra. 'Hair going grey, you know the kind of thing; he dresses well – oh yes, he has a bit of a limp and uses a walking stick. The well-bred company director type – I rather liked him actually, the little I saw of him ... it only goes to show how wrong you can be, doesn't it?'

'It does,' Morton agreed. 'Have you seen him recently?'

'Let me think,' said Myra, crossing her

legs higher up than ever. 'It was just before I went away this week, I've just come back from the country, you know... It must have been on Thursday, yes, that was it.'

She had been about to mention that little matter of Sam, but decided it might be unwise, especially if Essard turned out to be some kind of a crook after all.

'We weren't really friends,' she said. 'Just neighbours.'

'What about the other two?' said Morton. 'There was a Richard Bonner and a girl living there as well – did you know them?'

'Not really,' she said. 'I saw them in the lift and met them coming in and out, but I don't think I ever spoke to them, you know, beyond good morning and so on, just being polite. The girl was quite attractive in a way, I suppose ... twenty-three or so, dark hair and smart clothes. She didn't seem to have any job, and neither did the young man – I didn't care much for him, I must say, one of those brash young men who act as though any woman over thirty must be in her dotage.'

Not like Hugo Essard, Morton thought to himself.

'That was Richard Bonner,' said Morton. 'Did you ever hear the girl's name?'

'No. But somehow I don't think they were married – that was just an impression I got, I always assumed Essard must be the girl's uncle.'

'You might well be right,' said Morton gravely.

'Inspector,' said Myra, 'do tell me, what is this all about?'

'We don't know,' said Morton, which was much nearer the truth than Mrs Myra Foster would have believed. 'Wednesday night you spent here, Mrs Foster – it was the last night before you went away?'

'Yes. Why?'

'Did anything out of the ordinary happen that night? Anything you can remember?'

Myra shook her head, frowning, hesitating. Uncrossing and recrossing those gorgeous legs didn't help her now because Morton's eyes were on her face, although she thought he was smiling a little.

'Don't be alarmed,' he said gently. 'I'm asking for your help, anything you can tell me will be in confidence, you know that, don't you?'

'What sort of thing do you mean?' she said.

'Did you hear the sound of a shot coming from the flat above that night?'

'A shot? You mean a gun? Was somebody shot? I didn't hear it.' Myra wasn't pretending now, she couldn't disguise her nervousness. 'Was somebody shot?'

'Some time recently a gun was fired upstairs, in the hall,' said Morton. 'We don't know when and we don't know yet that anybody was shot.'

'You've asked Hugo Essard?'

'They've left, Mrs Foster, all three of them.'

'Oh,' she said, 'that was sudden, wasn't it?'

'Very,' said Morton.

Hesitantly, she said, 'I didn't hear any shooting, not that...'

'But there was something, wasn't there?' he said gently.

'I don't know,' she said, 'I don't know if it's worth mentioning – the morning I was going away, last Thursday, I found a leather case in the cupboard out there in the hall. It wasn't mine, and I'd never seen it before, and I just couldn't think what it was doing there. It was locked. Quite a good case, I'd say. I was in a hurry so I put it in my wardrobe on the top shelf, and when I looked for it today it wasn't there.'

'Anything else missing?' said Morton.

'Not a thing. I just don't understand it.'

At a nod from Morton, Sergeant Pritchard got up and went out.

'Who has a key to the flat beside yourself?' said Morton.

'Nobody,' she said. 'I'm a widow, Inspector, I live here alone. When the cleaning woman comes I'm here and I let her in.'

Pritchard came back. 'There's no sign of a forcible entry.'

'It's odd, isn't it?' said Myra. 'I've been trying to think what could have happened – I didn't imagine it, there was a case and now it's gone.'

She reached across to her handbag and took out a small key-ring. 'I never leave these around, nobody could have borrowed the door key, Inspector ... so how did they get in?'

'It can be done,' said Morton.

'What an unpleasant thought,' she said.

'Can you recall who has visited you here recently? Just before you went away? Essard was one of them, wasn't he?'

'I let him in,' she said. 'And I saw him out – he couldn't have put the case in or taken it out, it was after he'd gone that I found it in the hall cupboard...'

'And the night before that?' said Morton quietly.

'I didn't tell you Essard had been here,' she said.

'Not friends, just neighbours, you said.' Morton was smiling. 'But he did visit you here, and you rang up to invite him for a drink.'

'I thought he was all right,' she said defensively.

'Anybody else you can think of?'

'No,' she said. Then, a little defiantly, 'I have a number of friends of course, but none of them could possibly be concerned in this, the idea's too ridiculous, I mean, it wouldn't make any sense–'

'The case made sense to somebody,' said Morton. 'Somebody put it where you found it and somebody took it away when you weren't here, perhaps it was one and the same person. It wouldn't be too difficult to get in here and remove the case in your absence, what really interests me at this point is how and when and by whom it was put in your cupboard – how often would you go to that cupboard, Mrs Foster?'

She shrugged. 'Not regularly, it's difficult to say... I was looking for some golf clubs, and it was sort of hidden behind them.'

'So you can't really say how long the case might have been in the cupboard.'

'No,' she agreed. 'But nobody came here with that case, I'm sure of that … it's not exactly the kind of thing my visitors would have with them – I mean, it was a business case, rather expensive too … my visitors are social, Inspector.' She gave him a charming smile.

'This must be very distasteful for you,' he murmured apologetically, while Sergeant Pritchard thought – may the Lord forgive you, Inspector Charlie Morton, you are about to con the lady.

'We have reason to believe that a crime had been committed,' said Morton with disarming gentleness, 'connected somehow with the flat above yours, and the people who have been living there – I'm afraid it's very vague as yet, and we do need help, your help.'

'Anything,' said Myra Foster warmly. 'I'll give you all the help I can…'

It took Morton another fifteen minutes of discreet prodding before the matter of Samuel Harris was disclosed.

'It was quite amusing, really,' Myra said. 'Nobody in the world could ever take Sam for a dangerous criminal, he's really rather a pet and not very bright, and there he was outside my door just after he'd left … sort of arrested by Bonner and the girl and Essard, they thought he'd been acting suspiciously, they said, and they wanted to know if I knew him. So just for a joke I pretended I didn't know him ... not very sporting of me, perhaps, but it was only a joke.'

'Did Harris think it was funny?' Morton's face was expressionless.

'I'm afraid not, he was quite angry at the time. That was why Hugo Essard came down the next morning, he wanted to get in touch with Sam and apologise for the mistake. I told him it wasn't necessary, but he insisted.'

'So you gave him the address,' said Morton. 'Where does Harris live, Mrs Foster?'

'Porchester Walk, 14b,' she said, not at all so happy now.

'Do you know if Essard did in fact call on Harris?'

'No,' she said. 'I don't know. I haven't seen Sam since I've been back, he'll probably look in for a while this evening, if he's not still cross with me.'

He ought to twist your neck, Morton thought. 'And what does Harris do for a living?'

'I don't know,' said Myra, her uneasiness increasing. 'Nothing much ... he never has much money. I – I haven't known him all that long to tell you the absolute truth. Inspector, do these details of my private life really concern you? I'm ready to co-operate and all that...'

'Please,' said Morton winningly, 'do me one last favour ... please ring Harris, now, will you do that?'

She was very doubtful. 'But what am I supposed to say to him?' she asked. 'Invite him over here to meet two policemen? He won't thank me for that, Inspector.'

'We won't be here,' said Morton. 'I promise you that. We won't embarrass you.'

'All right.' They watched her dial, and all three of them listened to the unanswered *burr-burr*. When Myra put the phone down she looked relieved. 'What else would you like me to do?'

'Nothing,' said Morton, rising. 'You've been very helpful, Mrs Foster.'

'If Sam calls tonight,' she said, 'shall I tackle him about the case?'

'Better not,' said Morton. 'We'll be in touch with you later in the evening.'

'Do,' she said very politely. 'What a strange business this is.'

'I doubt if we know the half of it yet,' said Inspector Morton. 'Do you happen to know the name of the agents who handle the flats here?'

'Prestwick and Herkomer, in Gloucester Road,' she said. 'You can phone them from here if you like.'

'Thank you,' said Morton.

It was close to tea-time now, but the agency kept open late on Saturdays, and Morton learnt that the flat in question was on a long lease to the widow of a Colonel James Harrison-Drury, and that she had permission to sub-let since it was her custom to spend longish periods with her married children; it was all quite regular and in order, and the agency understood that Mrs Harrison-Drury was spending the summer in the South of France ... the current tenants? The agency had no knowledge, Mrs Harrison-Drury managed that on her own account ... but it was hoped that there had been no kind of trouble?

Inspector Morton assured the clerk it was purely a routine enquiry. And knew very well that it wasn't being believed.

Then he and Pritchard drove across to Porchester Walk, under the arch and down the cobbles. Morton rang the bell at 14b, and they waited. Morton rang again, long and loud, they could hear the bell ringing inside the flat.

A young man who had been apparently snoozing behind the wheel of a blue Volkswagen showed signs of life; a swarthy young man in a white shirt open at the neck, his sleeves rolled high, his wristwatch glinting in the sun as he leaned out to see them properly. He started his engine, but didn't drive away.

'That bloke looks interested,' said Pritchard softly, and began to stroll over to him. The young man withdrew his head and got into gear in a noisy hurry and shot off, swinging round under the arch. Pritchard noted the number. Their own car was facing the wrong way, and by the time they had driven round the block and came out again to the arch there was of course no sign of a blue Volkswagen.

'So we aren't the only ones with an interest in this Samuel Harris,' said Morton. 'I look forward to meeting him.'

A general alert was put out for the Volkswagen, and two hours later it was found nicely parked near Grosvenor Square, empty and wiped clean of prints, and by that time Morton and Pritchard had already been through the small dossier on a Samuel Harris.

'Nothing but small stuff,' said Morton.

'He could have lifted that case,' said Pritchard. He looked at the picture attached to the file. 'I wonder if the lady with those nice legs could identify him? Or would she be too coy?'

'Go and try the picture on her,' said Morton, 'and keep your eyes off those legs.'

'I'm a married man,' said Pritchard.

'That's what I mean,' said Morton.

Pritchard was back inside an hour. 'That's her boy friend,' he said. 'She was very upset, but she promised to ring us if he turns up.'

'He won't turn up,' said Morton. 'So we have to find him. We haven't had anything on him for over a year now, but he won't have strayed far from London. It shouldn't be a long job. We've had the Volkswagen checked, it belongs to the Argus Hire people, according to their records it's on hire to a firm in Victoria, the Eastern Export-Import Company – one room and a phone, there's nobody there now of course and there'll be nobody there on Monday either ... pity we scared that chap – your trouble, Wally Pritchard, is that you look too much like a copper.'

'Permission to speak, sir,' said Sergeant Pritchard.

'I know, I know,' said Inspector Morton, 'it's your rest day, but let's find this Sam Harris first. You and me and the rest of the Metropolitan.'

TEN

The mohair suit had been restored to him in good condition and at a fancy price. A sunny week-end lay ahead, and Sam felt he had the world by the tail. He was fireproof and he'd money to toss around. He needed company.

He watched the bird in the bar for some time before moving in. She was sitting alone, making one drink stretch out, looking as though she had a problem she didn't like. Young enough, blonde, tight yellow pants and a white jersey. He didn't think she was waiting for anybody because she didn't look at her watch. Just sat there at the bar cuddling her glass, frowning.

He fetched up alongside and gave her a polite smile. She nodded. Close to she didn't look as young as he had guessed, about thirty, but still all right for an evening. He offered her a drink.

'Are you by any chance trying to pick me up?' she said.

'Just a friendly gesture,' said Sam. 'Please yourself.'

'I'm a respectable married woman,' she said, 'and to hell with it, I'll have a Bloody Mary.' She swung round on her stool to face him and crossed her legs, and those pants were too tight to accommodate anything but her under them. She looked Sam up and down. 'I'm Kathy, who are you?'

'Sam. Isn't your husband around?'

She snorted. 'Him, he's in Rome or Athens ... don't be frightened, he won't arrive until the middle of next week.'

'What a crying shame,' said Sam, 'leaving you all alone.'

She smiled briefly. 'You're as big a liar as he is.'

'Can't fool you,' said Sam. 'I think you're gorgeous, all the same.'

'I'm bored,' she said with sudden bitterness. 'I'm sick up to here ... you'd better go and find yourself another playmate, Sam.'

Her drink arrived.

'I'll stick around,' said Sam. 'Cry on my shoulder any time you like, no obligation.'

She shuddered as the drink went down.

'You need food,' said Sam.

'Couldn't face it,' she said.

'Nothing like a good nosh-up,' said Sam, 'to start with.'

'You have improper designs on me,' she said. 'To start with what, Sam?'

Sam grinned, and she didn't spit in his eyes. Later he steered her into the dining-room, and she discovered she had the remains of a healthy appetite, which cheered them both enormously.

Her husband was an airline pilot, she said, and it was clear she didn't enjoy being left behind for days on end.

'And when he comes back he's too damned tired to be any good,' she said. 'Chatting up those Italian bits... I get what's left and it's dam-all after being married for five years– I sound like a proper bitch, I know.'

'Rugged,' said Sam sympathetically. Airline pilots had it made, everybody knew that ... birds all over the place. In like Flynn. Me too, he thought.

She had her own car, a white Triumph Herald; they lived in a modernised cottage a couple of miles away. Why didn't she get a job? She was too lazy, she said, she didn't like getting up in the mornings – said with a lazy smile that suggested all manner of private ideas to Sam.

When he walked with her out to her car she made the move.

'I make a good cup of coffee,' she said, 'if you're interested.'

'I'll get my car,' said Sam.

'No.' She opened the passenger's door. 'I'll see you get back.'

It was against Sam's principles not to allow for an independent retreat, but this looked all right to him, so he got in.

The cottage stood alone in a quiet lane. Plenty had been done to it so that it wasn't a cottage any more. Worth ten thousand quid of anybody's money in that area, Sam guessed, and it was pretty snazzy inside as well. They didn't bother with the coffee after all.

Kathy helped him to shunt the twin beds together and she had the delicacy to remove the picture of her husband from the bedside table – a bad-tempered bastard in uniform with a big spread of whiskers. Sam was happy to think he was safely on the other side of Europe. And he had been right about those yellow pants, Kathy whipped them off and the sweater and there she was, a bit bony round the hips, but ready and willing.

She made him share the shower with her, which was a giggle for Sam because it wasn't in his line, but she insisted, and built it into a right piece of business like in one of those pictures Sam had paid a quid to watch when he was nothing but a lad and didn't know what it was all about.

She was a very inventive and active dolly, and he began to understand why her old man might find her a bit too much after a trip to Capri or Naples or what have you. After all, a bloke has to get some sleep.

Kathy kept him awake for a long long time. Kind of in a frenzy, making up for lost time, cussing and moaning and chewing lumps out of him and calling him Freddie.

They both didn't stir until well after midday, and when she shifted round in the twisted sheets to face him she didn't at first know who the hell he was, her face all blotchy and her eyes puffed. Then she remembered and sat up and reached for him.

Sam skipped nimbly out of bed and found a white towelling wrap, Freddie's no doubt.

'Come over here, you little red-headed goat,' said Kathy, stretching out one arm, 'we haven't finished–'

'You ought to get yourself doctored,' said Sam. 'I'll go down and make that coffee you were on about last night.'

Kathy lay back on the pillows and said a naughty word. Down in the kitchen Sam found the stuff he needed, and abundant evidence that Kathy was no housewife – the kitchen had all the modern gear, but there were messy bits and pieces all over the place, and a heap of dirty dishes.

He made the coffee and took it up on a tray. She was asleep. He drank his coffee and helped himself to a cigarette from the box by the bed. If he roused her she would expect to start all over again, and he didn't fancy that. In the bathroom he found a razor and shaving cream, Freddie's no doubt; he shaved very quietly and got into his clothes. Kathy slept on, and he imagined he wasn't the first week-end partner she had entertained.

He could think of no suitable farewell message that she might care to read. Out in the sunshine the Triumph Herald stood by the garage, but she had taken the keys. He had to walk, not his favourite means of travel. All of four miles, in a hot sun. Loads of fast Sunday traffic and nobody inclined to stop and offer him a lift. So he walked.

Hugo Essard was not enjoying his Sunday either, he had a new warder, a virile young man bursting with health and energy, who hustled him into the bathroom and slapped him on the back when his operations appeared too dilatory. He said his name was Stanley and he promised Essard that he was going to relish every moment of their association. Chop chop, old son, get a move on, time is wasting.

The fastidious Essard suggested that he might be allowed to shave and take a bath.

'You have to be joking,' said Stanley, and thrust him cheerfully back into that dreary little room. Later on, much later on, the door was unlocked and Essard braced himself for the interrogation he knew must be coming, it was a modest breakfast on a tray, with Stanley.

'Keep your strength up, you'll be needing it,' said Stanley, and stood inflexibly over him while he ate.

When he had finished, Essard said, 'I insist on knowing how long you intend to keep me here.'

'Where is Bonner?'

'I honestly have no idea,' said Essard.

'That's how long we will be giving you free board,' said Stanley. 'You're rubbish, we know that. We want Bonner, to start with.' He took the tray and went out.

Somewhere in the distance church bells were ringing. Essard stood and gazed out of the window at the garden below, a tidy suburban garden with fruit trees and nice patches of lawn; every now and then he heard the scream and thunder of jets; he knew he must be somewhere south, they had probably taken him by a roundabout route last night – it could be Wimbledon, or New Malden.

Stanley came out into the garden with a deck chair and some papers, he saw Essard and gave him a happy salute, as though they were comrades, then he settled down with the papers, facing Essard's window. Nothing else happened all day. Food, just enough. A very long day.

Late in the evening they took him downstairs, into the same room as before. Leo Grussmann was there again, very spruce.

'I suppose it's no use saying how much I protest,' Essard began.

'No use at all,' Grussmann agreed. 'What have you remembered since we met?'

'If you want Bonner I can't help you, I don't know where he is now – if I did know I'd tell you ... and I know nothing of his business.'

'The first part of your answer is true,' said

Grussmann. 'Perhaps– I don't think you would risk yourself to save him. But I am also sure you know what he was doing, you shared that flat, with the girl – obviously you knew what he was about, you were part of it, a very minor part, Essard, the front man – you will stay here with us until you recall some details.'

'If you are so sure that I am some kind of a criminal you should hand me over to the police,' said Essard. 'You have no authority here over me.'

'We have all we need,' said Grussmann gently. 'Don't deceive yourself, you are not the stuff of heroes, this is not a matter for heroics, you have been in this for money– I could offer you money, twice what they have been giving you, but we have better uses for our cash ... remember what I called you last night, Essard, a mercenary saboteur, the lowest of the low.'

'I insist on being taken to the police,' said Essard. 'I don't know what you're talking about, if you wish to press charges against me there is a correct way to do it.'

'I wonder if Harry Voyses had the chance to say as much?' said Grussmann, 'and would it have made any difference? Take him away, let him shave before I send for

191

him again – he is a great gentleman for what is correct.'

Essards' legs were shaky as he stood up. 'You are nothing more than bandits,' he said and he was unable to prevent his voice sounding shrill. 'I had nothing to do with Voyses – I wasn't even there.'

Grussmann smiled. 'You sound like all the good middle-aged Germans – they never heard of concentration camps or gas ovens, so they just couldn't have happened. Take him away, Stanley, before he provokes me beyond repair.'

Stanley took Essard upstairs and locked him in, and the simple fact that Stanley had nothing to say to him did nothing to comfort Hugo Essard. Downstairs Stanley went back to Grussmann.

'What do you think about him?' said Grussmann.

'He doesn't seem frightened enough yet,' said Stanley.

'Whatever they are planning, I don't think it's too immediate, or he'd be more jittery, more scared of being worked over... I'll be watching him – I could beat something out of him, if you prefer–'

Grussmann shook his head. 'Let him think about it, a few more days on his own ... let him think nothing will happen, just remind him now and then about Voyses. I don't think he has very much nerve.'

So began another long lonely night for Hugo Essard. And yet another day. Stanley didn't lay a hand on him. He brought him his food, watched him shave and let him even change his clothes from the stuff in Essard's cases. With the utmost good humour he made him do press-ups until he flopped on his belly on the floor.

'You'll never last the course,' said Stanley sadly. 'You'll fold up as soon as we start, you'll be a poor substitute for Harry Voyses.'

Essard lay panting on the floor, his flabby muscles shaking.

'We'll have to toughen you up,' said Stanley. 'I'll be back in forty minutes and we'll have another try.'

Essard wept from sheer despair and exhaustion, but it did him no good.

On Monday afternoon Sam Harris drove to Chiswick and down the side road near the river where he had followed the Mini all the way from that Army camp. From the back he couldn't see much but the high wall and the double doors, and a bit of the house. He did a careful tour of the front. It was a short road, no more than fifteen houses, and all big ones. It was the end one that interested him.

There was a short drive, but shrubs hid most of the house from the road. The gate was shut. There was no number, just the name 'Endymion'. The house next door was occupied by a bunch of doctors – there were four names on brass plates fixed beside their gate, and while he sat in his car on the other side of the road people were trickling in and out.

If only he had a phone number for 'Endymion' – he could whisper a few disturbing words to Ric Bonner, start him sweating about all that dangerous dope on Lockerton Camp and the armoury ... and the black leather case. He could jack the price right to the top ... he didn't think Ric Bonner could be the boss, Hugo Essard with the dud leg? Or another big brain across there in that house?

He drove up the road to a phone booth and tried Directory Enquiries. There was no Richard Bonner or Hugo Essard listed. He quoted the 'Endymion' address.

'I know he's stopping there,' he said, 'but I haven't got the number–'

There was a pause, and the operator repeated that neither Richard Bonner nor

Hugo Essard was shown as a subscriber, and through the glass panel Sam saw Sophie walking along the pavement towards him, looking smart and expensive and not a bit like a rough dolly who would toss a man around and like it. Sophie sure enough and by herself. The operator was still squawking some crap, but he put the phone down and turned his back as Sophie passed.

Then he slid out and sat in the car and watched her for a few seconds. She couldn't try any of that judo stuff in the street in broad daylight, all the same he took the screwdriver with the wooden handle out of the glove compartment and put it on his side of the seat out of sight, and he drove slowly after her.

She took no notice at first when he was level with her, like anywhere else, Chiswick has its quota of kerb-crawlers even on a fine afternoon.

'Having a nice walk, Sophie?' he called. That stopped her. She sauntered over, peering, frowning.

'My God,' she said quickly, 'it's you – you do get about, don't you? What are you after this time?'

'That's a good question,' said Sam happily.

'Have you been following me?'

195

Sam just grinned. 'Well I'm not here by accident, baby doll.'

'I see.' She looked cautiously about. They had that bit of the pavement to themselves. And Sam knew what was coming next. So he stretched across and opened the door for her. She slipped into the seat beside him. She smelt good and those legs were on show, right there to hand.

'Sam,' she said softly, 'we'd like to talk to you, you're a sensible man, and you're smart – you found out where we are, that was really smart of you.'

She put one hand on his thigh and now she was leaning close to him. Sam brought up the screwdriver and rapped the back of her hand.

'Don't maul me, baby,' he said.

She swore and sucked the back of her hand. 'You didn't have to do that.'

'I got a good memory,' said Sam. 'You make another move I don't like and I'll stick this in your ribs– I want the phone number of that house back there, the place you just came from.'

She blew on her hand. 'You're a rough little bastard ... why do you want the phone number?'

'I might want to talk to somebody,' said

Sam, 'about a black leather case.'

That rang a bell, Sophie stopped bothering about her hand. 'We could drive back there now,' she said.

'I'm not that crazy,' said Sam.

'Are you on your own?' she asked. 'Is that why you're scared to come back with me?'

'I've got something your lot want,' said Sam, 'and I'm the boy who says how it's going to be handled, who's your boss?'

'Just ask for the Doctor.' She opened her bag, took out a small diary and scribbled a number and tore the page out. 'You won't be able to get him until Wednesday or so,' she said.

'I'm in no hurry,' said Sam, putting the paper into his pocket.

'I suppose we couldn't get in touch with you?' she said. 'In case the Doctor thinks it advisable–'

Sam just grinned at her. 'Midday Wednesday, and your bloke had better be available or I might just get other ideas.'

'About that case,' she said, 'you've got it safe?'

He patted her thigh. 'Wouldn't be much of a giggle if I lost it, would it?'

She got out of the car and walked back the way she had come, and she wasn't loitering.

Sam took off at speed. It would be healthy to keep away from London for the next few days.

ELEVEN

When the whisper reached Chopper Roberts that the fuzz were looking for Sam Harris in such an urgent manner, Chopper was interested and gave the matter plenty of thought. Sam was a louse all right, but he had never amounted to anything big before, and this had to be big or the fuzz wouldn't be giving it all the heat – they were asking about Sam all over the place ... the crime boys and the Special Branch, making London a bleeding menace to a bloke who had his living to get.

Chopper had been brooding over the way Sam had done him dirty, the cocky little conniver ... all that smart stuff when Chopper had lifted that bleeding case for him, leaving him with the dirty end of the stick, that was Sam Harris all over.

Chopper thought there might be a bob or two to be picked up here. The heat was on for Sam, and Chopper guessed it might have something to do with that case – Sam was such a tricky bastard, and that case had been hot, must have been – or Sam wouldn't have been so steamed up.

It grieved Chopper beyond endurance to think that he'd had the case and Sam had diddled him. Might have been a bundle of loot inside.

So the bird whose flat he'd taken it from, she might be offering a reward for information, in confidence, of course. Chopper knew who she was, there'd been letters in the flat – Mrs Myra Foster.

One afternoon Chopper rang her. Was the lady interested to hear something about a black case that had been taken from her flat? Chopper used his normal husky furtive whisper, and Myra had him repeat himself before she got the idea, then she said she was definitely interested – when could they meet?

'It's a bit delicate,' said Chopper. 'I'll have to make some arrangements … and I don't want no cops in it, you got that? Private, just you and me… I know plenty about Sam Harris, you wouldn't believe it, lady.'

'I think I would,' said Myra sweetly. 'Why don't you come here? We could have a nice private talk – I didn't get your name–'

'I never gave it,' said Chopper, dead cunning. 'Would you be thinking of some kind of a reward like? I got information, just between you and me...'

'I'm sure we can come to some agreement,' said Myra. 'When will you come?'

'Tonight,' said Chopper. 'Half past seven, okay?'

Just before the appointed time he gave the building a careful check; there wasn't a police car parked outside, and he had his story ready – nobody could prove it wasn't true, nobody but Sam Harris and he wasn't likely to be around.

Myra let him in, gave him a drink and listened, while Chopper gave a version that fitted some of the facts: he knew Sam, they were mates from way back, and he had met Sam with a black leather case in his car and Sam had been acting nervous about it, wouldn't say where he'd got it or what was in it.

'Proper jittery he was,' said Chopper, 'so I knew it wasn't his ... did you lose a case like that?'

'I did,' said Myra.

Chopper shook his head at the baseness of some people.

'Sam nicked it, that's what,' he said.

A door opened and Sergeant Walter

Pritchard came in. Chopper knew what that meant and made a dive for the door. But he hadn't a prayer. Pritchard hauled him back. Chopper gave Myra a very dirty look.

'Don't say it,' said Pritchard. 'Where's Sam Harris?'

'Bleeding well find out,' said Chopper with some bitterness. 'You can't trust nobody these days…'

Much later that evening in an interrogation room, Chopper had told them what he knew, although he was still sticking to the main outlines – that Sam had pinched the case from the flat, and that Chopper had met him afterwards by accident.

They had Chopper's record, which inclined none of them to believe Chopper's version in full – Chopper was a very handy lad with a lock, always had been, and the lock on Mrs Foster's door would have been a doddle for Chopper. Chopper denied it with much indignation.

'You won't find no prints of mine in there,' he said. 'I'm clean and you can't prove otherwise, not this time … the last I seen of that case Sam had it in his car, last week, on the Thursday it was, and he never told me where he was going … what was in the bleeding thing anyway? The Crown Jools?'

They kept at him – what had Sam said to him and what had he said to Sam and so forth. Chopper sweated and became more furtive than ever, and he heartily wished he had never brought the matter up – with his experience he ought to have known better than to let himself get tangled up with the fuzz. The bastards never believed a word you told them when you had a record.

He was expecting to be booked on suspicion, but they let him go, with a warning that they would be keeping an eye on him, and if he put another foot wrong... Chopper assured them he was as white as the driven snow and knew very well that nobody believed him, then he was allowed to scuttle out into the night.

They had a man on Chopper's tail, which didn't alarm Chopper unduly – if they thought he was going to lead them to Sam Harris they were wasting the taxpayers' money. Wherever Chopper went for the next few days the shadow was near at hand, which seriously embarrassed Chopper's operations with parked cars and their contents in West End squares, and he was obliged to pass his time in public libraries and other unprofitable areas.

One thing had become clear to Inspector Morton and his associates: Sam Harris was somehow in possession of something that might be of importance to somebody else, a black leather case that had mysteriously arrived in Mrs Foster's flat and just as mysteriously had disappeared – into Sam's keeping. So Sam Harris had to be picked up, and soon.

They had built up a pretty fair picture of his normal movements, he was a sociable character when he had the money, and the clubs and pubs were being checked, and Mrs Myra Foster's flat was under strict surveillance – by now it had been established that Sam had been more than just a casual visitor, although Mrs Foster had never admitted as much.

'Somehow it all began there, in that building,' said Morton. 'Harris was a regular visitor, and in the flat above we have Essard and Bonner and the girl – all of whom moved out in a hurry.'

On the instructions of his superiors he was talking once again with Leo Grussmann, over cups of coffee in a neutral location, and once again he was finding the conversation one-sided, with himself doing most of the talking.

'Pity you have no pictures of them,' said Grussmann. 'They seem to have vanished, don't they? But you'll find this Harris ... odd to find small fry like him mixed up in this.'

'That's the way it goes,' said Morton.

'You don't happen to have a spare picture of Harris I could take?' said Grussmann. 'One of our people might spot him for you.'

Morton took out a copy of Sam's picture and passed it over. 'We've spread them about, somebody must see him.'

'Unless he knows and is keeping quiet,' said Grussmann.

'Or somebody else has got to him,' said Morton. 'We've had one dead body?'

Grussmann shook his head. 'We have had no dealings with this man, Inspector, that I can promise you ... he is not another Harry Voyses, I have never seen this man before, or heard of him.'

When they broke up Morton left with a feeling that Leo Grussmann still hadn't told him all he knew, and there was nothing much he could do about it beyond reporting it to his superiors. Grussmann was entitled to show the CD plate on his car, which made him no ordinary citizen.

Grussmann showed the picture of Sam

Harris to Mrs Voyses.

'He has never been here,' said Mrs Voyses, 'and I never heard my husband mention the name of Samuel Harris. Who is he?'

'We don't know,' said Grussmann, 'yet. But we will find out.'

Mrs Voyses looked hard at the picture. 'I would not trust that one,' she said.

'You are probably right,' said Grussmann.

'Was he concerned with the death of my husband?'

'We hope to find that out,' said Grussmann.

With Hugo Essard he had better luck, because by now Essard was depressed and reaching a state of desperation. Lack of fresh air and exercise, except for the strenuous gymnastics Stanley put him through on the dusty floor of that dreary little room, were having a cumulative effect, and all the while Stanley was hinting at enormous tribulations that were coming soon to Essard. They had cut his food down to the very minimum. No cigarettes now, no papers, almost no conversation. Hugo Essard had become a Thing, and of no great importance.

'You know him,' said Grussmann.

Essard pretended to give it some thought.

'Possibly. I meet a number of people, but I don't really remember this one.' He was trying to make the connection between Grussmann and this Harris, it didn't seem likely, but there had to be a connection.

Had this Harris after all been working with Voyses that disastrous night? Harris had been on the stairs just after they caught Voyses … and the case hadn't been found – and they had let Harris go, Ric Bonner had let him go, Bonner had been so damned sure his decisions were the right ones.

'Start remembering,' said Grussmann. 'I can wait all night, when did you see this man last?'

'Why do you want him?' said Essard.

'He's a petty crook,' said Grussmann, 'but you know that, don't you? What did you use him for?'

Essard laughed. 'If you can believe that you can believe anything – what possible use could we have for that kind of man?'

'You use all kinds of trash,' said Grussmann. 'Tell me about Harris.'

'The simple truth is that we found him lurking on the stairs outside our flat one night last week,' said Essard. 'We thought he might be a burglar, but he satisfied us he wasn't so we let him go.'

'That's stupid enough to be true,' said Grussmann.

'It's true,' said Essard stolidly, 'even if you don't believe it. What do you want him for?'

'A good question,' said Grussmann. 'Remind me to give you the answer one day.'

Doctor Aristide Apian had been summoned to a special conference, to a palatial pink and white villa in the hills behind sunny Tripoli. Having at last evicted the foreign intruders from the former RAF base at El Adem and elsewhere, Libya was now able to take her rightful place in the brotherhood of the United Arab Front ... and to hell with the Israeli aggressors and all the corrupt governments who afforded them help and protection, spreading their dirty propaganda against the rights of true Arab nationalists and their legitimate aspirations.

There were delegates representing all the main European groups, reporting on their spectacular activities in Rome, Paris, Amsterdam, Zurich, Athens, and so forth. Israeli-owned properties had been blown up in half a dozen cities; aircraft had been destroyed or hi-jacked ... at one period some of the major air lines had been refusing to fly aircraft into Israel, which had been applauded as a considerable victory for the cause. A freighter, outward bound from Marseilles with engineering parts for Israel, had been sabotaged in mid-ocean, with a gratifying loss of cargo, and most of the crew.

One of the more recent exploits had been the kidnapping of the only daughter of a high-ranking Israeli official from her finishing school in Switzerland, which would bring home to her father the unwisdom of the inflammatory speeches he had been making in Tel Aviv. It had been agreed that this was to be the first of a kidnapping campaign, to be carefully thought out and executed with ruthless efficiency. A committee had been set up to exchange information and to correlate plans.

Aristide Apian had been the least vocal in that enthusiastic assembly, which grieved him, because he was quite the youngest there, and, to his own way of thinking, obviously the most talented. To have had nothing concrete to offer had been mortifying, and his colleagues from the group based in France had been openly derisive about the lack of activity on the London front. What was wrong with the clever boy? Had he lost his nerve? London was wide open, everybody knew that, the British were notoriously sloppy over political activities – perhaps somebody else should take over Apian's generous budget, somebody who could show some results.

Apian had been forced to listen to much comment in the same critical vein. He was not liked, because it was thought that he had risen too fast and too quickly. So now let him show them what he could do. Or get back behind a safe desk in Cairo, and leave the real work to men who were not too frightened to do it.

Shukulin was there, in an advisory capacity, from Big Brother in Moscow; a stolid smiling-faced man, acknowledged as the King Daddy of saboteurs, to be listened to with respect, a man whom even Aristide Apian admired.

On the afternoon of the second day of the conference, when Apian should already have been back in London, Shukulin invited him into a private room and went over what Apian had arranged as his contribution. The notion of talking their way into a British Army camp appealed to Shukulin, it was the kind of thing he had done himself.

'Grenades,' he said, 'keep grenades in your mind, for use in crowd work, official processions, public demonstrations ... invaluable and most effective in all circumstances, they require no skill and no accuracy, from the windows of an upper floor or behind a wall ... you follow me?'

Aristide Apian did.

'Find me a street map of London,' said Shukulin, 'and I will show you where I would work if I were with you to get the maximum effect. We would need details of any future events that might interest us, public appearances... London is busy in the summer, is it not?'

Apian had to agree it was.

'There are the sporting meetings,' said Shukulin, 'so very dear to the British, my friend – you will know that as well as I do ... the horse racing, the tennis games at Wimbledon, each may offer you a suitable target ... you will give it thought?'

Apian said he would.

'Secure your ammunition first,' said Shukulin, 'then devise the best use for it. I look forward to hearing about you – never count the cost, act quickly and where you are least expected ... and where you will create the most confusion.'

Wholesale slaughter, that was Shukulin's theme, and he elaborated it while Apian listened and was privately glad that he wasn't acting under Shukulin's directions. The map of London was produced, and Shukulin pencilled in the likely areas – he knew more of London than Apian had suspected, he was, after all, the Master in the construction of booby-traps.

'When I think of London,' said Shukulin, 'I remember the words of the old Prussian, Blucher – what a city to sack. Almost I envy you…'

When Sam Harris rang the Chiswick number at midday on the Wednesday as arranged, Sophie answered and said she was sorry but the Doctor was still away and they had been unable to contact him – which was strictly true. Would Sam like to talk to Ric Bonner who was there and available?

'Tell him to get knotted,' said Sam. 'I'll try again same time tomorrow and your Doctor better be around.' Then he rang off, a little peeved at being taken for just another mug.

If this Doctor character was the boss he was the one Sam was going to deal with, and in the meantime Sam kept away from London. Sophie had seen his car, and she would have passed on his number, so he drove across to Godalming, did some sniffing around and came across a party who wanted to exchange a Morris Traveller for something newer – a middle-aged lady teacher was easy for Sam, she fancied the Eleven Hundred when Sam shaved the price, omitting to tell her he still owed three hundred on it to the finance company; she even drove with him to the bank where her cheque was turned into real money for Sam, the balance being two hundred and ten.

The Traveller had been carefully used and well serviced, and Sam drove back well content. When he had fixed up a deal with this Doctor bloke, he'd be looking for a Jag at least, cream with red leather. That lady teacher was due for an unpleasant shock, but she was old enough to know what a wicked world it was. Next time she'd be more careful.

Around the pub Sam had been keeping a sharp eye open for that Kathy, but she didn't show up, which was all right with Sam. He thought of ringing Myra, just to tell her what a bitch she was, but decided she wasn't worth the bother. There were plenty of birds about a damn sight younger than Myra.

The future was beckoning with rosy fingers, for Sam Harris. He wasn't scratching about for a crust any more. He was going to be Big.

On Wednesday evening, Ric Bonner made a quick run down to the village. At half past seven Fred Halley hadn't appeared by the bridge, so Bonner gave him ten minutes, then drove up to the bungalow and rang the bell. Inside kids were squawking, and mum was leading off at them.

With her burgeoning stomach heaving under a damp apron, Mrs Halley opened the door just a little. 'He's sick,' she said. 'He can't see nobody... Doctor says he's gotta stay in bed.'

'I'm sorry,' said Bonner. 'I hope it's nothing serious?'

Mrs Halley sniffed and shifted the hair that straggled over her face. 'Nervous breakdown, that's what the Doctor says ... if he don't get better they'll have him in the hospital I shouldn't wonder.' She didn't sound as though she would regret that much.

'That's too bad,' said Bonner. 'I suppose I couldn't see him just for a minute.'

'You leave him be,' said Mrs Halley, and slammed the door. Presently the sounds of juvenile distress increased, as Bonner walked down the path – a nervous breakdown on the part of Fred Halley made sense

214

all right; at least it would keep him away from the camp over the week-end.

Inspector Charles Morton was reading through the reports of the various sightings of Sam Harris that had been coming in. They were as expected: he had been seen buying petrol in Tottenham; he had been drinking with a red-headed woman in a pub in Islington; he had stayed two nights in a lodging house in Camden Town; he had been seen on the top deck of a bus in Greenwich. And so on.

They had been through his place in Porchester Walk; from the very few papers there they knew Sam Harris almost never paid a bill; most of the correspondence started with the formula: 'Dear Sir, Unless...' Final demands in red.

For a petty crook with few resources, he was proving highly elusive – which meant that he had changed his habits of late, or else he had run into something too big for him – and had got himself eliminated.

Mrs Myra Foster had a succession of plain clothes men more or less camping in her flat, waiting for Sam to call her. At first she had enjoyed the novelty of the situation, some of the detectives being young and quite presentable; but they all seemed to share an inability to be aware of Myra's delectable presence, which irritated her and made it a bit of a bore at the end. And Sam Harris didn't call.

On the Thursday Sam delayed his call until the afternoon. Let them do the worrying. He got Ric Bonner and he didn't sound happy right from the start.

'I want the Doctor,' said Sam. 'I don't talk to the office boy–'

'He's on a trip,' said Bonner. 'Listen – I'll meet you anywhere you say–'

'–Not a hope,' said Sam. 'I know you – you'd turn up with an army.'

'It wouldn't be like that,' said Bonner earnestly. 'The doctor's abroad, that's a fact, I'm not trying to put you off. He'll be back soon and he'll want to see you, talk business – that's what you want, isn't it? Make a deal? No funny stuff? You keep the cash in the case–'

'–I already got it,' said Sam. 'It's the other stuff I'm thinking about – see what I mean?'

'Yes,' said Bonner soberly. 'We'll have to fix up a meeting to talk it over.'

'I'm ahead of you,' said Sam. 'I fix the

price. You wouldn't want that case to get into the wrong hands, would you? Be kind of explosive, hey?'

Sam laughed. Bonner saw no joke.

'I'm selling and you're buying,' said Sam, 'so I only deal with the boy who has the cash, and that isn't you, old cock ... and don't you forget it.'

'We can set up the details,' said Bonner. 'The Doctor will agree to anything I fix when he comes back – what's the price?'

'Five thousand,' said Sam. And there was a pause.

'You don't think small, do you? You're squeezing us–'

'Put it to your boss,' said Sam. 'I'll be in touch again some time tomorrow.'

'You do that,' said Bonner, and he didn't sound too cordial.

TWELVE

Aristide Apian returned in the middle of Friday morning. He listened to Bonner and Sophie, and his first concern was how much did the others know – Fenna and Timmins and Tessie Raikes?

'I haven't told them,' said Bonner. 'As far as they know it's still on for tomorrow.'

'It is,' said Apian.

'Too dodgy,' said Bonner.

'You can withdraw,' said Apian. 'We can do it without you – where is Essard? Hasn't he been here?'

'I think Hugo had cold feet,' said Sophie. 'He's not at his club, we don't know where he is.'

'No matter,' said Apian. 'He is not important now.'

'I think we ought to put it off,' said Bonner. 'This Harris character knows about it ... we don't know that he won't talk.'

'So we will have to make sure that he does not talk,' said Apian. 'His interests are commercial, he wants money. That should make him simple to handle.'

'I doubt that,' said Bonner. 'He's smart.'

'I have thought that from the first,' Apian reminded him. 'I have thought all along that he must be a professional – he refused to deal with you because he would know that you have no authority–'

'–I'd wring his damned neck if I got my hands on him,' said Bonner. 'He's messed this up all right.'

'We know he has not been to the police,' said Apian, 'or they would have been here days ago. Agreed?'

Bonner nodded.

'He is in this for the money he hopes to make out of it.' Apian smiled across at Bonner. 'Like yourself.'

Bonner met Apian's gaze – something must have happened to Apian while he was off on that mysterious trip, he was tougher, more dangerous.

'I still think it would be a mistake to go on,' said Bonner. 'We should wait a bit.'

Aristide Apian was remembering Shukulin's flattering interest … and the derisive attitude of some of the others. He was not going to lose this chance.

'We cannot wait,' he said.

'That's what I think too.' There was a

mocking smile on Sophie's face, and it was directed at Ric Bonner. 'Surely we ought to be able to cope with this little man – he's on his own, that's obvious... I don't think he's all that lethal.'

'Stop sounding heroic,' said Bonner. 'You won't be taking any risk, so shut up.'

'I think I could handle Harris, in the right circumstances,' said Sophie.

'He'll take the money and drop us in the dirt,' said Bonner.

'Of course,' said Apian, 'if we give him the opportunity, but I don't intend to do that. He is greedy, we will let him over-reach himself.'

'You'd better explain,' said Bonner.

'Are you still with us?'

'I'm ready to listen,' said Bonner. And Apian told him.

When Sam rang again in the afternoon he was gratified to hear that at last he was talking to the Doctor, who sounded quite apologetic for not being available earlier. Sam announced his terms, the time and the place, and the Doctor said they would suit him admirably.

'Just you and the cash,' said Sam. 'If anybody else shows up, or if I don't like anything you do, the deal's off – got that?

And remember, I'll have some of my crowd inside and outside, we can play it rough if we have to—'

'I take your point,' said Apian, 'but this will be a simple business transaction, there will be no violence.'

'Five thousand,' said Sam, 'and cheap at the price.'

Aristide Apian laughed softly. 'You drive a hard bargain, my friend, but it will be as you wish.'

'I'll have it in fives,' said Sam.

At half past seven that evening Sam sat in the saloon bar of a pub he had chosen with special care – there was a police station less than fifty yards down the road, the landlord was a retired Sergeant of the Metropolitan force, and the local fuzz used the place regularly. Normally Sam wouldn't have given the pub a second look, but tonight it afforded protection, in case this Doctor bloke tried to lean on him. There was a secluded rear entrance, and Sam had parked the Morris Traveller there.

Aristide Apian pushed back the swing door, looked quickly round the bar, and walked over to where Sam sat by himself at a table.

'Mr Harris?' he said politely.

'Where's the money?' said Sam. He had the black leather case on his lap.

'In a case in my car ... you would like us to make the exchange in here?'

Sam nodded. 'Get it.'

'It's rather public,' said Apian. 'Won't you want to count the money? It comes to quite a pile—'

Sam tapped the case. 'Maybe I've made some copies, maybe I'll send them to one of the papers – or the coppers ... so don't try to twist me, chum.'

Apian nodded thoughtfully, turned and went out. A moment later a uniformed constable came in and came over to Sam.

'Outside,' he said, and pulled Sam to his feet.

'Hey,' said Sam, 'what's up with you? I haven't done nothing—'

'Out,' said the constable, shoving Sam over to the door.

The landlord was in the other bar; there were at least a dozen clients in the saloon, but none of them came from the local station, they just happened to be law-abiding citizens who saw that the constable was well in control of the situation.

Sam protested and wriggled, but they

were outside on the pavement, and the constable knew how to handle a reluctant subject – clutching the case, Sam was given the bum's rush across to a black Mercedes with the rear door open and the engine running. He was tossed in headlong, Apian received him, the constable climbed in and the car surged off.

Momentarily speechless with rage and indignation, Sam watched the helmet and tunic being hastily removed just as they were passing the police station, and they weren't stopping.

'You're a bunch of dirty bastards,' said Sam, and was slapped smartly on the mouth.

'Five thousand pounds,' said Aristide Apian. 'You must think we are stupid.' He was holding the black leather case. 'You have had all the profit you are likely to get from this, my friend.'

Sam said some bitter words and got himself slapped again so that his eyes watered, and he shut up. Slapping wasn't all he was facing, he knew that.

They took him back to Chiswick, down to the kitchen where Harry Voyses had paid his final account, and this time there was no need for any extreme treatment: Sam was very ready to oblige with what they wanted to know, and he had no trouble convincing them that he had been on his own and that nobody else knew what was in the black leather case, but he failed utterly to convince them that he was just a harmless interloper.

'A silly little man,' said Aristide Apian indulgently. 'You have put us to a deal of trouble, now you are an embarrassment, we must consider what we are to do with you.'

Sam didn't much care for the sound of that. 'I won't give you any trouble,' he said earnestly. 'I can keep my trap shut ... honest–'

'You disappoint me,' said Apian. 'I have been taking you for a professional, and all the while you were just a dirty little back-street scavenger.'

'Now wait a minute,' said Sam, 'that's a bit harsh ... after all, look at it my way– I thought we made a deal, I mean–'

'You are a fool,' said Apian. 'It should have been clear to you that I was not going to give you five thousand pounds for what was mine.'

'You're smart,' said Sam bitterly. 'So what happens now?'

'If you expect to be at liberty you are a bigger fool than I thought.'

Sam let that one pass.

'You are out of your depth,' said Apian. 'And you are on your own, fortunately for us – if you had told somebody else your position would be different, and we could not afford to hold you for long here ... this is much too big and important for scum like you.'

'You're one of those bomb-throwing bastards,' said Sam. 'I know about you lot...'

Aristide Apian smiled at Ric Bonner. 'There speaks an English patriot.'

'A little rat,' said Bonner, 'from the sewers.'

'So what does that make you?' said Sam. 'You're not even a bleeding Arab like this ponce here, you're English–'

Bonner hit him hard, and toppled him off the chair. Sam was slow getting up. Sophie had been watching, smoking, remembering Harry Voyses sitting in that chair and what the end had been on that occasion.

Sam got to his hands and knees. Less than an hour ago he had been laughing, he had it made – the biggest tickle of his career, five thousand smackers as good as in his fist. Painfully he fitted himself back into the chair.

'This I am going to enjoy,' said Bonner.

'Leave him,' said Sophie, 'leave him, Ric – he's not Voyses–'

'He's worse,' said Bonner savagely, and once more Sam was on the floor, with his head singing and blood running from his mouth. This time he decided to stay down, and so Bonner used the sharp toe of his shoe with his hands contemptuously in his pockets. Sophie left.

Eventually, bored at the lack of resistance, Bonner lugged Sam into a room near the kitchen; it had formerly been a larder, there were shelves round the walls, a cold stone floor, and one small window too small and too high in the wall to be any use to the prisoner. There was still a lingering smell of old cheese and sour vinegar, and there was no furniture, one unshaded bulb.

As Bonner shot the bolt in the door, Apian said, 'You feel better about tomorrow now? Your mind is clear?'

'It'll be all right,' said Bonner.

'We must remove him, when this is over,' said Apian. 'It is lucky for us he is a greedy little man… I thought he would over-reach himself, and I was right – all this might have been avoided if you had taken him in the first night you saw him. However, there has been no damage.'

'Pathetic when you think of it,' said Bonner, 'rubbish like that in there trying to hold us up.'

'Money makes fools of most men,' said Apian. 'Samuel Harris is an opportunist, but he will not be one much longer.'

They went upstairs to Apian's room to go over the final plans for the movements next morning, and this time Sophie was concerned: she would be driving a Dormobile to the meeting place in the clearing near Lockerton village, with changes of clothing for the party, civilian clothing; they would transfer the cargo into the Dormobile, and abandon the 'army' vehicles. Then the five of them, with camping gear strapped on the roof rack, would be just another party of holiday makers – three men and two girls.

'Essard should have been in touch before this,' said Apian.

'Too gentlemanly to get his hands dirty,' said Sophie. 'He will appear when it's all over and done with, so I have to do his job–'

'–You'll manage,' said Bonner sourly. 'Any half-wit can drive a Dormobile.'

'Thank you, sweetie,' said Sophie, smiling maliciously. 'Then you can drive it back.'

'This is childish,' said Apian. 'We must work as a team, it is essential.' On his desk

227

was the black leather case, with the folder. 'We will check the timing once again so we will all know what to expect, each of us…'

Sam Harris was in darkness. The floor was chilly, breathing was hell, and he had swallowed some of his own blood – it didn't taste good. Even in a police cell they gave you a mattress to lie on. After a while he was able to grope about and find the light switch, and his situation looked dismal indeed when he could see where he was. A couple of mice scampered across the floor and disappeared into a hole in the wall, at least they had each other and somewhere to go.

There was blood down the front of his shirt and the mohair jacket would never be the same again. His habitual optimism had abandoned him, and he was devoutly wishing he had never set eyes on that blasted black case.

Squatting desolately on the floor he hugged his bruised ribs … he'd been so right about that Ric Bonner the first time, a right nasty bastard.

After a long sad brood, he made himself go through the motions of checking the one window, and it gave him no joy; it was right out of his reach, a little square of dirty glass that looked as though it hadn't been opened for years; even in his better and more agile days he couldn't have done anything with it; and the door was solid.

Clobbered. He had two cigarettes left. His bladder urgently needed relief. He banged on the door. He shouted. He swore until his voice cracked. Then he had to use one of the corners.

After the alarm Sam Harris had caused in Feltham, Ted Fenna had to find other premises for the vehicles, which suited him because he swore he wasn't going to spend any more evenings where he might get himself beaten up, not even for the thirty quid extra a week. After some careful sniffing about among his associates in the car-breaking world, he found the right place, even better than the one they were vacating – on the edge of Bermondsey, under the arches of a disused railway viaduct; next door was a vast rubbish tip, and the Old Kent Road was nice and handy. It was a neighbourhood where nobody inquired too closely into your business, a neighbourhood where 'hot' vehicles were transformed overnight, or where cartons of desirable items – like cigarettes or television sets or similar nonperishable goods in popular demand – found a temporary refuge after being 'lost in transit'.

When he had finished with Apian, Bonner picked up Tessie Raikes and they drove across to Bermondsey; she was ready to stop on the way for a few snifters, but he told her this was going to be a sober night for all of them.

'So we'll kick it around afterwards, right?' said Tessie. 'Me and you, Ric ... we'll make some sweet music.'

'We'll do just that,' said Bonner.

'Everything okay?' She put her hand on his leg. She just had to keep touching him, leaning against him so that one of those bulging breasts nudged him ... as though he might forget she was there, and after all those nights of sharing her bed he needed no reminding. Tessie was too much of a bonus for a man with other things on his mind, Tessie thought a bit of sex solved it all.

He'd be glad when it was over and he could ditch her. She was still yakking on about this holiday she imagined they were going to have together in Majorca. Fun in the sun, for God's sake! Acres of toasted Tessie to be coped with. He let her prattle on.

Ted Fenna was waiting for them, so was Timmins, and the two vehicles were ready.

Timmins slapped the Humber's bonnet. 'Wish we were travelling tonight,' he said. 'Be nice to get it over with.'

'Nervous?' said Bonner, giving him a sharp look.

'Me?' Timmins laughed, a shade too heartily. 'You must be joking, chief – I'm looking forward to it!'

'That's fine,' said Bonner. 'Keep off the booze until this is finished– I don't want you hung-over tomorrow morning.'

'Not a drop,' said Timmins, coming to a mock-attention, heels clicking.

'Three cheers for Dad's Army,' said Fenna. 'Mr Bonner, I worked us out a route, missing out all the main roads – it'll take us a bit longer, but I reckon it's worth it ... have a look.'

He unfolded a road map and traced a route with a pencil, meticulously estimating distances and times. 'The main roads out of London are plain murder on a Saturday, so we dodge our way round most of them ... we don't want to get stuck in a jam.'

'We don't,' Bonner agreed.

'Three hours and thirty minutes I reckon,' said Fenna. 'No sweat, easy driving... I'll lead until we get near the camp, okay?'

'We'll have to be ready to move off from here at eight sharp,' said Bonner. 'Let's have a final check on the uniforms, Tessie.'

She unlocked a cupboard and brought the uniforms out one by one and distributed them – correct and used working dress for everybody, except 'Driver' Fenna who would be in denims suitable to a slightly scruffy soldier who had lost his week-end pass to drive a truck.

'Captain' Bonner and 'Sergeant' Timmins had medal ribbons and the insignia of the Wessex Division; Tessie would be driving in shirtsleeve order – she held the khaki skirt against herself and hoped she'd get into it without a disaster, her hips having spread just a little, she admitted strictly to herself, but she expected to get by on her legs.

Bonner declared himself satisfied. 'Any questions?'

'When do we expect the big pay parade?' said Timmins. 'I could do with an advance right now.'

'Payment in full tomorrow, when we deliver the goods back here,' said Bonner. 'That was the agreement – the money is all right, it's up to us as a team – if we do a smart job tomorrow there'll be something extra, and I'm not talking about the odd fiver either … there won't be any snags over money.'

'So this time tomorrow I'll be laughing,' said Timmins.

'We'll all be laughing,' said Ric Bonner.

THIRTEEN

'You're not trying,' said Stanley. 'You're just a great lump of blubber ... drag those guts up off the floor and let's have some action ... hup-hup-hup!'

The repeated schedule of press-ups were having less and less effect on Hugo Essard, he was collapsing more and more quickly, sobbing on his belly on the floor, unable to raise another twitch from his quivering muscles, his purple face running with sweat, and all the time, whenever his gasping lungs allowed him to get any words out, he was insisting that he didn't know where Ric Bonner was.

He was so exhausted now that a couple of shaky thrusts on his forearms had him face down on the floor, weeping at himself.

'You're useless,' Stanley told him quietly, 'you're dross, you're a heap of junk, old man... I wouldn't soil my hands on you...'

Late on the Friday night, after a particularly bad day, when Essard had been too beaten to eat anything, Stanley let him kid himself that he was going to be allowed a long night's rest, and he had watched Essard crawl on to the bed and fall into a deep immediate sleep, broken only by the spasmodic twitchings of his legs and the loose skin around his mouth and the whimpering breathing. The room smelt of old sweat and exhaustion.

Leo Grussmann was downstairs. Everything seemed to be at a standstill, and in his bones he had the feeling that they were about to miss something that should be happening.

'Let me cut him just a little bit,' said Stanley.

'No,' said Grussmann. 'That brings us down to their level, and I don't want that.'

'Harry Voyses,' said Stanley.

'I haven't forgotten,' said Grussmann.

'An eye for an eye,' said Stanley. 'It is a good precedent. His heart isn't too good, he's all flabby now... I have another way, it might kill him, but there will be no mark.'

Leo Grussmann said nothing. Stanley went into the kitchen and made them both some black coffee, and he said nothing to disturb his chief's train of thought.

Presently Grussmann said, 'We have to bear in mind the possibility of having to hand him over to the police, it may have to come to that ... from what I hear they are making little progress.'

'If he won't talk to us he won't talk to them,' said Stanley.

After a while, Grussmann stood up. 'The coffee was good.'

'I will do my best to see he does not die,' said Stanley.

'Call me,' said Grussmann, and went out.

In the small hours Hugo Essard was roused to find the stinging pain in his arm hadn't been part of any dream. Stanley was bending over him, in one hand he held a syringe.

'Wakey-wakey,' he said. 'Rise and shine...'

Essard found himself sitting on the edge of his bed far more wide awake than he would have thought possible, breathing deeply and regularly, all tiredness drained off.

He had gone to sleep in his pants and vest; there was a strange tingling sensation in his fingers.

'What do you want?' he said. 'What have you done to me?'

'A little injection to freshen you,' said Stanley, 'to revive that old stamina ... get over and stand facing the wall.'

Woodenly Essard limped over, and listened

to the instructions from Stanley, then he supported himself with the tips of his fingers on the wall, and his feet were moved further and further back so that all the weight was on those fingers, and when he tried to cheat and use the palms of his hands Stanley was beside him to correct him.

The injection had heightened his sensitivity, and he felt the increasing strain right up his forearms ... when he collapsed and slid to the floor, Stanley heaved him upright, and they began again.

It was a slow process. Later he had to support the weight of his leaning body on the tips of his two forefingers only, and keep his head clear of the wall.

'You are now smelling something fierce,' Stanley told him. 'Can't you smell yourself, old man? Just give a thought of Harry Voyses, he had it a lot worse than this...'

Essard's breath came loudly through his nostrils, his game leg, where the ankle had been broken in his youth, began to give under him more and more frequently, but Stanley was a willing lad and heaved him up to begin again.

Occasionally, and by way of contrast, he revived Essard with buckets of cold water before yanking him to his feet.

Essard had one hope left, that he would lose his senses, but it didn't happen, he remained acutely aware of everything, and Stanley continued to handle him like a firm and patient nurse who intends to stand no nonsense. There wasn't a bruise on Essard's sodden body to show for all his weariness.

It was morning when he spoke, although he had lost all notion of time, the curtains were still drawn and the light was on.

Huddled on the floor, his saturated vest wrinkling over his heaving belly and his face turned into the wall, he lifted a hand in surrender, and Stanley was there kneeling beside him.

'There is a house in Chiswick,' said Essard hoarsely. 'You should go there ... for God's sake I can't stand any more...'

Stanley dumped him up on the bed. Essard keeled over and fell with his face mumbling into the pillow, and it took all of Stanley's ingenuity to rouse him and prod the words out of him so that they made sense.

He held Essard upright by the shoulders, shaking him, the first really violent thing he had done – let Amnesty International make a case out of that, he thought – how the wicked Israelis torture prisoners!

'Talk, you slob!' he whispered.

Essard talked, his head wobbling and his eyes out of focus, slopping the words out as though unable to control his mouth. He had held out longer than anybody had the right to expect of him. He was now beaten, at the end of a wearisome line, too sorry to care any more.

Stanley bounced downstairs and got on the phone to Leo Grussmann. 'I got it all and it didn't kill him,' he said. 'Listen to this..'

Grussmann relayed it all very promptly to Inspector Charles Morton. 'You have been complaining about lack of co-operation,' he said. 'I have a surprise for you–'

'I'm listening,' said Morton.

Doctor Aristide Apian was conducting a seminar with three of his best and most promising young men, none of them much over twenty and all so much alike in appearance that they might have been triplets. Full of zeal for the cause, they were proud of having been selected to carry the message into London.

With the aid of a large-scale map, Apian was demonstrating how vulnerable some public occasions in London were, and what a dramatic effect grenades would have in the hands of determined men, such as themselves. Each of the three would be given a sector to study.

'Make yourselves familiar with the streets and the buildings to which we will give attention. Trafalgar Square, for instance, that is where they hold their protest meetings ... and the Embassies unfriendly to us.'

Apian smiled as he added: 'I am arranging an ample supply of modern grenades, from the British Army.'

There were wide smiles that grew wider as he finished: 'Without permission, of course.'

Three police cars drew up in front of 'Endymion', while another car sealed off the rear. Apian's seminar came to an abrupt halt.

The three young men rashly attempted to resist the entry of the police; one of them had a revolver and was prepared to be heroic with it, he managed to get off a couple of shots, one of which broke the glass in the fanlight over the door, and then the invasion was on, and Sergeant Walter Pritchard slammed the young man against the wall with his forearm cutting off the young man's breathing.

'I know you,' said Pritchard, 'in a blue Volkswagen in Porchester Walk – you didn't wait to be introduced...' He allowed the young man to resume breathing, only just.

Aristide Apian had retreated to his study on the first floor, but he had omitted to lock the door in his urgency to get to the phone, and they burst in on him while he had the phone in his hand.

Inspector Morton took it from him and replaced it. 'Are you Aristide Apian?'

'I am,' said Apian, stiffening. 'By what authority are you here? I have diplomatic status, I insist on talking to my Ambassa-dor–'

'All in good time,' said Morton politely. 'You are not in your Embassy now, we are police officers, and I am Inspector Charles Morton of the Special Branch–'

'–You have a warrant for this intrusion?' Apian snapped.

'Now what do you think, sir?' said Morton. 'Would you like to read it?'

'I have diplomatic immunity,' said Apian. 'This is police persecution–'

'We are strictly neutral,' said Morton, 'except of course when we have reason to believe that a crime is being prepared or has been committed.'

'Neutral!' Apian sat down at his desk. 'I must be allowed to report this to my Ambassador immediately, it is my right!'

'You haven't asked what crime I'm talking about,' said Morton. 'Aren't you interested?'

'I have nothing to say until I have reported this outrage to my Ambassador.'

Morton was watching Apian's face. 'Go on,' he said quietly, 'why don't you ask who told us?'

Apian placed his hands flat on the desk and looked across the room, as though what was happening had nothing to do with him.

'Hugo Essard,' said Morton. 'I don't think your Ambassador is going to be terribly pleased to hear about you – plotting to steal weapons and so forth from an Army establishment, now that hardly fits your role as a diplomat, quite apart from the use you were going to make of the stuff ... any comments, Doctor Aristide Apian?'

'I have diplomatic immunity,' said Apian automatically. 'You can do nothing to me.'

'We'll have a very good try,' said Inspector Morton pleasantly enough. 'Now you just sit quiet while we check the rest of the place.'

It was a uniformed constable who heard

the muffled banging while he was going through the kitchen. He traced it and un-bolted the door, and a very weary and un-fragrant Samuel Harris emerged.

'Gawd,' he said, 'I never thought I'd be glad to see one of your lot–'

The constable wrinkled his nose and peered over Sam's shoulder. 'You have some dirty habits,' he said. 'Are you Samuel Harris?'

'That's right,' said Sam sourly. 'I been locked in there since last night ... you blokes took your time getting here.'

'Less of your lip,' said the constable. 'They want you upstairs, so jump to it, lad.'

'Jump nothing,' said Sam. 'I'm bruised all over.'

He waddled over to the sink and rinsed his face under the tap; he could do nothing about the dried blood on his jacket and shirt. Then he permitted the constable to escort him up to Apian's study.

He gave Apian a very dirty look indeed and pointed at him dramatically. 'That's the bloke,' he announced, 'the lousy bastard had me knocked off last night – you wouldn't credit what they did to me...'

'Mr Harris,' said Morton, 'we have been looking for you. I am Inspector Morton, and

I think you have some explaining to do, about a black leather case, and why you didn't turn it over to the proper authorities – you follow me?'

'Well now,' said Sam, 'that's a good question, Inspector…'

'It had fifteen hundred pounds in it,' Apian interrupted. 'That was why he kept it. You should be charging him with theft, if you know your business. He stole fifteen hundred pounds, Inspector, so let us see some of your famous British justice working–'

'He's off his onion,' said Sam easily. 'Listen, Inspector, don't you pay any attention to him – I got the real dope – there's a gang of them going to bust into some Army camp–'

'–Lockerton,' said Morton. 'We know, Sam, it's all been taken care of.'

'Well that's all right then,' said Sam, his confidence returning. 'No harm done–'

'I wouldn't say that.' Inspector Morton's voice was gentle, but Sam knew what that tone meant when a copper used it. 'We still have things to talk about, you and I. But not here, Mr Harris … my office will be much better, don't you agree?'

Sam didn't, but he knew it would make no

difference. That bleeding leather case … and the fifteen hundred quid … and why didn't you turn it over to the police, Mister Samuel Harris? You couldn't win.

At fifteen minutes after midday the Humber drew up at the main gate to Lockerton Camp. In a khaki skirt that was just a little too short to meet strict WRAC regulations, Tessie got out and went over to book them in. She gave the Corporal on duty a flashing smile that made his day, along with those eloquent legs she had on show – there hadn't been a better-looking driver through those gates for months. Those officers up at HQ had all the luck.

When the Captain on the rear seat of the Humber glanced across with a bored air, the Corporal gave him a smashing salute with some of the good old M.P. stamping, and they were passed in, the truck following.

The Corporal watched them turn the first corner. Behind him in the main Guard-room his Sergeant spoke into the phone he had been holding: 'just come through, sir … all in uniform … yessir…'

'I'd give a month's pay to be up there in the Armoury,' said the Corporal.

'Bloody sauce,' said the Sergeant, 'driving in here like that…'

In the Armoury the duty Corporal was deep in the *Daily Mirror* when he had to scramble to his feet at the appearance of a Captain followed by a Sergeant and a bloke in denims.

'Morning, Corporal,' said Bonner briskly, 'is Lieutenant Dunne about?'

'Off playing cricket, sir,' said the Corporal. 'Anything I can do for you, sir?'

'Good man,' said Bonner, surveying the room. 'I'm from Div ... we've put in an indent for some gear, don't suppose it will have reached you yet?'

'Nothing's come through, not to my knowledge,' said the Corporal. 'What was it you were wanting, sir?'

'Let me see now,' said Bonner. 'Grenades, with fuses ... thunder flashes – oh, and some of the new CS gas jobs ... can do? We've laid on a field exercise and the Brigadier wants to make it realistic, toughen the troops up ... y'know the thing ... teach them to keep their heads down, and all that.'

Bonner gave a superior Staff officer's smile. The Corporal scratched his chin doubtfully.

'Well I dunno, sir,' he said, 'what with the officer being away and that–'

'If it's the paper work that's bothering

you,' said Bonner airily, 'I'll pop into the Mess and have a word with Major Bamford on my way out – he'll be in command with the Colonel on leave, right?'

'Yessir...'

'Splendid,' said Bonner. 'The Brigadier would be frightfully annoyed with all of us if we didn't get what he wants ... and we can't have that, can we, Corporal?'

'Nossir.'

'That's fine, Sergeant, carry on ... and don't forget the fuses ... thank you, Corporal.' Bonner nodded and sauntered out.

'Let's get weaving, lad,' said Timmins, and beckoned to Ted Fenna. 'We don't have all day...'

'Field exercise with live ammo,' said Ted Fenna scornfully. 'You ever heard of such crap?'

'You'll find yourself back on jankers, my lad, if you don't watch it,' said Timmins severely. 'Let's be having you...'

The Corporal unlocked the ammunition store, they followed him in, and Timmins selected what they had come for. He didn't do any of the carrying, he was a Sergeant, and Sergeants don't work up a sweat when there's a Corporal and a private soldier handy.

Sitting behind the wheel of the Humber, Tessie pretended to be taking no interest in the matter. 'Piece of cake,' Bonner murmured, 'nothing to it ... we're getting everything ... another couple of minutes and we'll be on the way out.'

'Can't come soon enough,' said Tessie without looking at him. 'I'm getting my knickers in a twist, waiting here.'

When the crates had been loaded on the truck, Timmins stamped up and saluted. 'All correct, sah!'

'Excellent,' said Bonner and slid into the rear seat of the Humber. 'Easy now, Tessie,' he said, 'turn by the gymnasium, they'll follow ... don't hurry, it's all okay...'

In the Armoury the Corporal was on the phone, talking quickly: 'Grenades and fuses and CS gas, no weapons – leaving now–'

Rounding the last bend, they saw the barrier coming down across the road out, and a three-ton truck was backing to reinforce the barrier.

'Damn,' whispered Bonner, leaning forward, 'what the hell are they up to? Give them a toot, Tessie.'

Tessie sounded off, and nobody took any notice, so she had to brake. 'What now?' she said over her shoulder.

'Turn left, up the Mess side road – left, you stupid cow – *left!*'

'Stupid cow yourself,' she said, pulled the Humber round too late to make a neat turn, and Ted Fenna, following up too closely, nipped the rear of the Humber and shunted it on to the grass verge sideways, rattling Bonner and Tessie hither and yon.

Bonner swore.

'Somebody put the mockers on us,' said Tessie. 'We're all boxed in, look–'

Troops were appearing from all directions, armed troops with weapons at the ready, converging on the two vehicles.

'A piece of cake!' said Tessie bitterly.

Bonner was glaring about, slapping the seat. 'I don't get it – they were waiting for us – I don't get it!'

'You will, boy, you will,' said Tessie. 'Let's hear you talk us out of this one.'

A plump Major advanced, flanked by large subalterns, and said: 'All right now, out with you.' And that was effectively that.

Sophie waited in the clearing with the Dormobile. They were late, ten minutes, twenty minutes – she began to agitate herself. Then she heard the sound of an engine coming up the lane, so it was all right.

A jeep arrived, with two soldiers with red caps, very serious and official and quite polite.

'You have to come with us, miss,' one of them said. 'You might as well, we've got the others at the Camp.'

Sophie looked at the Dormobile, shrugged, and went with them.

They were in Inspector Morton's office, and he had just put the phone down.

'All gathered in,' he said. 'No casualties – they were after grenades and CS gas.'

Leo Grussmann pursed his lips. 'That suggests wholesale operations … a grenade makes a mess and doesn't have to be accurate, in a crowd for instance.'

'We found some interesting items in Apian's place,' said Morton. 'Annotated maps of London, the Embassy has begun to make heated noises, but I imagine they'll cool off when they hear the full story.'

'Terrorism on a large scale,' said Grussmann. 'Nice, in London of all places … that won't do their public image much good.'

'Quite,' said Inspector Morton. 'They'll shed Doctor Aristide Apian very smartly, I shouldn't wonder.'

'So Harry Voyses was on the right track after all,' said Grussmann, 'when he went in after that case—'

Sam Harris had been listening, sitting on the edge of his chair, and trying to pretend that he was there of his own free will to assist the police, which was far from the truth.

'Voyses?' he said. 'Was that the bloke I saw on the stairs that night? Fat little feller with a bald head? What happened to him?'

'He's dead,' said Morton. 'They killed him.'

'Listen,' said Sam urgently, 'I reckon they did it in that place in Chiswick – last night, when Bonner was roughing me up, that bird Sophie, she said to him that he didn't have to be tough because I wasn't Voyses ... and he said I was worse and then he really clobbered me.'

Sam glanced hopefully at the Inspector, like an honest citizen. 'I'll swear to that in any court you like, Inspector.'

'Good,' said Morton genially.

'Always ready to help the police, that's me,' said Sam. 'Okay if I go now?'

Morton smiled. 'Not quite – were you trying to make a deal with them, Mr Harris? Was that why you kept the case and didn't

251

tell anybody? Us, for instance?'

'Me?' said Sam. 'I wouldn't do a thing like that.'

'I'm so glad for you,' said Morton, pleasantly, 'because technically that would make you a party to the conspiracy, an accessory before the fact in other words ... which would make you as guilty as they are, you understand?'

Oh Gawd, here we go again. Sam nodded and began to sweat ... and he still had over a thousand quid to spend.

'Now let's get it all down in a nice tidy statement,' said Inspector Morton. 'Begin at the beginning, and don't leave anything out—'

Sam promised he wouldn't. But he did, naturally. You can't change the habits of a lifetime.

The publishers hope that this book has given you enjoyable reading. Large Print Books are especially designed to be as easy to see and hold as possible. If you wish a complete list of our books please ask at your local library or write directly to:

Dales Large Print Books
Magna House, Long Preston,
Skipton, North Yorkshire.
BD23 4ND

This Large Print Book, for people
who cannot read normal print,
is published under the auspices of

THE ULVERSCROFT FOUNDATION